ISLAND ESCAPES

CAITLYN LYNCH

Caitlyn Lynch

ISLAND ESCAPES

Finding Cory

Olivia Stratten wasn't thinking about romance when she accepted a job as marketing director for a resort island on Australia's Great Barrier Reef. She just wanted to get far, far away from New York and her ruined career. Activities director Cory Gillette is the kind of man who is hard to resist, though, and Olivia finds that maybe she doesn't want to resist anyway…

The Reluctant Billionaire

Sunfish Island Resort seems like the perfect place for Jace Hunter to recover from a serious illness… as long as nobody figures out his family owns the island.

Meeting Nessa, a psychiatrist turned bartender, Jace comes to realize that maybe the society life he's been living isn't where his future happiness lies.

Caitlyn Lynch

Copyright © 2017 by Caitlyn Lynch

All rights reserved. This book or any portion thereof may not be reproduced or used in any manner whatsoever without the express written permission of the author except for the use of brief quotations in a book review.

Other Works by The Author

DANA'S DUO

RANGER HEAT SERIES
1. FIRST SUBMISSION
2. SECOND SURRENDER
3. THIRD THRILLS

ELEVATOR ENCOUNTERS SERIES
1. ELLIE'S ENCOUNTER
2. JULIET'S ROMEO
3. THE BEST MAN FOR LEAH

SHENANIGANS PRESS ANTHOLOGIES
STOCKING STUFFERS
RED HOTS
SUMMER HEAT

HALLOWEEN ANTHOLOGY (upcoming)

Caitlyn Lynch

FINDING CORY

Island Escapes Book 1

CHAPTER ONE

The incredible heat surprised Olivia as she stepped off the plane and walked down the steps to the tarmac. It was just like being slapped in the face with a hot, wet towel. She broke out in a sweat almost instantly and considered pausing to take off the jacket to her pantsuit, but the terminal was just a few steps away and the promise of air conditioning beckoned. Shouldering her laptop bag, she made rapidly for the doors.

Since she'd come in on a domestic flight from Sydney, she didn't have to clear international customs. After collecting her suitcase, she made her way to the greeting area and looked hopefully around.

Almost everyone who'd been on the flight with her were tourists, and they were making their way to several tour group and resort signs being held up around the area. Olivia bit her lip, wondering if she should head for the brightly colored sign proclaiming the legend SUNFISH

ISLAND RESORT with the tourists going in that direction, or if there was a different protocol for newly arrived staff.

Not seeing anyone holding up a sign with her name, she shrugged mentally and headed on over. A pretty Chinese girl holding the sign and a clipboard smiled at her, though the smile turned quizzical as she took in Olivia's designer pantsuit and high-heeled pumps, a far cry from the comfortable holiday wear the tourists sported.

"Hi, I'm Jill! Your name, please?"

"Olivia Stratten."

Jill glanced down automatically at her clipboard before her head snapped back up. "Wait, you're the new marketing manager!"

"I am." Olivia smiled.

"Welcome, it's lovely to meet you!" Jill shoved her clipboard under her arm to pump Olivia's hand enthusiastically. "Sorry we didn't have a specific sign for you—well, we did, actually. Rosie was gonna hold it but it turns out that her boyfriend was the co-pilot on your flight and it's turning around and going back to Sydney in an hour so she went to try and see him for a few minutes."

Olivia blinked at the sudden gush of information delivered in a broad Australian accent. She'd only been in the country for a week and still struggled to pick up all the words when the locals talked quickly. She was pretty sure she'd gotten the gist, though, and nodded.

"That's alright. I hope she got some time with him."

Jill rolled her eyes. "Guy's a prick with a girl in every town. I keep trying to tell Rosie, but she's blinded by the whole airline-pilot-glamor thing."

"That's still a thing?"

"Considering how much pilots get paid, yeah," Jill said with a wry twist of her lips. "Here she is now."

Olivia turned to see another young woman hurrying toward them. She was a little taller than Jill and about Olivia's height, brown-haired, and very tanned. Her white teeth flashed in her brown face as she smiled.

"Hi, you must be Olivia! I'm Rosie, the staff manager at the resort. It's lovely to meet you!"

Charmed by the friendly, unaffected greetings from two women Olivia guessed were both around her own age of twenty-nine, Olivia smiled back at them. "It's lovely to be here. So different from New York." She'd left home in chilly, dark October, when the city seemed shrouded in gloom as winter approached. Sydney had been quite a shock to the system, warm and bright, green with spring growth. North Queensland was *hot* and far more humid. When she'd looked out of the plane window as it came into land, the view had been all turquoise water and sand-rimmed tropical islands.

"I reckon," Jill said with a laugh in her voice, giving Rosie a glance Olivia couldn't interpret before she turned away to see to the tourists awaiting her attention.

"Jill's our guest relations manager," Rosie said, gesturing for Olivia to follow her. Grasping her suitcase handle, Olivia obeyed, and Rosie led her out of the terminal to a golf cart parked outside and helped her hoist her case into the back.

"We'd go on the bus with the others, but it's full. We've got a lot coming in off this flight." Rosie hopped into the driver's seat. "So I borrowed this off a friend at the marina."

"Is that far from here?" Olivia hung onto the side of the golf cart as Rosie mashed the accelerator pedal flat to the floor and they took off at a surprisingly high speed.

"Not at all! Only a couple of minutes!" Rosie zoomed past another golf cart, narrowly missing an oncoming minibus. Olivia gave up and shut her eyes.

"Oh come on, you're used to New York traffic. My driving can't terrify you that much!" Rosie snickered.

"You'd make a very good cab driver," Olivia agreed, cracking an eye open as they slowed. Seeing boat masts in front of them, she relaxed, realizing they must be at the marina. "Which is all I ever took in New York. Generally, the subway is much faster anyway, so I mostly rode that."

"I think I'll take that as a backhanded compliment," Rosie snickered. "Well, you can drive next time, if I'm scaring you that much. Jill never lets me drive…."

"I can see why, but I don't have a lot of choice. I've never learned to drive."

"Really?" Rosie looked startled at that before casting her a cheeky grin. "Well. Technically you don't need a license to drive one of the resort golf carts. I won't tell if you don't."

Olivia had to laugh at that, getting out of the cart. "Is this the boat?" She looked at the catamaran yacht they'd parked behind.

"No, no. This belongs to my friend. Thanks, Matt!" Rosie yelled at the boat before heading around to the back of the cart to heft Olivia's suitcase out again. "We're just going along there."

"Oh." Olivia felt quite foolish. Lovely though the catamaran was, and obviously valuable, it looked minuscule compared to the magnificent motor-yacht at which Rosie had just pointed. "Wow."

"The resort has three of those; we use them for airport transfer, inter-island transfer, and our own dive-and-snorkeling tours," Rosie informed her. "They're brand-new. The new owners bought them after they finished the refurbishment last year."

"Impressive," Olivia said, taking in the boat as they walked closer. "Several million dollars, I'd say."

"No expense spared," Rosie agreed with a nod. "Everything on Sunfish Island is like that. You'll see. But the island was run-down for quite a few years before the new owners bought it and spent a fortune to do it up."

"Which is why you need me." Olivia nodded. She specialized in relaunching refurbished hotels. She'd originally applied for the job assuming she'd be based in New York, but the resort owners insisted she needed to be on-site. They'd hired her on a full-year contract and paid all travel expenses, and accommodation was included. It was the job of a lifetime.

"That's right." Rosie nodded. "Hey! Cory! Get down here and help carry Olivia's suitcase!"

"God, you're so bossy," a deep voice rumbled with a laugh, and Olivia looked up to see a tall figure silhouetted against the sun, standing on the boat's upper deck. She blinked, dazzled by the glare behind him.

"This is Cory Gillette, our activities manager," Rosie said as the man vaulted over the rail. He landed on the lower deck in front of them before walking down the short ramp separating the boat from the dock. "Cory, Olivia Stratten, our new marketing guru."

"Nice ta meetcha," he rumbled before bending and picking up her suitcase as though it weighed nothing.

Olivia could only stare speechlessly as Cory turned and walked back onto the boat. He looked as though he'd just stepped off an advertising billboard; tall, blond, and blue-eyed, he had a deep bronze tan and shoulders so broad they strained the seams of his polo shirt. Her gaze slid down his back involuntarily as he walked back up the ramp with her suitcase.

Cory's ass in tight khaki shorts was so spectacular she barely heard Rosie's "Come on, let's get aboard before the guests arrive."

"Ngh," Olivia said somewhat incoherently, still staring, but Rosie promptly cut off her view as she headed up the ramp in front of Olivia. Still thoroughly distracted and trying to peer around Rosie to get another look at that incredible back view, she followed Rosie up the ramp without watching her footing.

Which turned out to be an epically huge mistake.

The ramp was made of a pierced steel grating, and with Olivia's first full step onto it, her spiked high heel went straight through and jammed. Thrown completely off balance, she teetered, clutched for a nonexistent handrail, lost her balance completely, and toppled head-first into the murky waters of the harbor. The last thing she heard before the surprisingly warm waters of the harbor closed over her head was Rosie's shriek of horror.

She might never have learned to drive, but she had certainly learned to swim. After a brief panicky flail, she righted herself and kicked back up to the surface, clamping her lips tight and holding her breath. Her head broke the surface and she heard....

Not more shrieks of horror, but a deep guffaw of laughter.

Cory was leaning off the boat, extending a tanned hand in her direction, and absolutely laughing his ass off.

Cheeks flaming, utterly humiliated, Olivia accepted the offered hand. It wasn't as though she had much choice, after all. As far as she could see, she had no other way to get up to the boat.

Despite his chortles, Cory pulled her up as easily as he'd carried her suitcase, his other hand hooking around her waist when he'd raised her high enough to lift her aboard and set her on her feet. Her bare feet.

"I think this is yours," he said through his laughter, bending down to pull her shoe out of the ramp and offer it to her.

"Those were Jimmy Choos," Olivia said pathetically, accepting the shoe from his hand even as she mourned the loss of the other one, now no doubt sinking in the silt at the bottom of the harbor.

Cody laughed so hard he had to sit down on the deck.

"You're such an asshole," Rosie was at least *trying* to suppress her giggles, and making a fair job of it, as she dealt a slap to the back of Cody's head. "Are you alright, Olivia?"

She blew out her cheeks, looking down at her ruined five-hundred-dollar pantsuit, the single shoe nestled in her hand. And then she blinked. "Oh my God. My bag!"

"You had a bag... your laptop bag!" Rosie stared at her in horror.

They both peered down into the murky water.

"How deep is it?" Olivia asked.

"About eight feet." Cory finally managed to suppress his laughter. "And no, I am not diving down to look for it."

Olivia shot him a fulminating glare. "Don't put yourself out. I'll get it myself." Handing Rosie her shoe, stripping off her soaked suit jacket and tossing it aside, she dived neatly off the edge of the boat.

CHAPTER TWO

"Now *that* I didn't expect," Cory admitted, peering down after her. "D'you think I should go in?"

"I think she wouldn't have dived in if she wasn't quite confident she could do it," Rosie said thoughtfully. "And frankly I think you'd be better served here to pull her out again when she comes back up."

Cory started counting under his breath, though, deciding that if Olivia hadn't surfaced after sixty seconds, he was going in after her. He'd reached fifty-four when her head broke the surface again.

"Did you get it?" Rosie called. Gasping for breath, Olivia nodded, holding the strap up in triumph. Rosie grabbed the bag while Cory hauled Olivia out again.

"There was no need for that," he chided. "Seriously, all your electronics will be wrecked already."

"I know that." She cast him a scornful look. "All my data is backed up to the cloud anyway. I just didn't want to lose my passport. It'd be an absolute pain to get a new one." Taking the bag from Rosie, she opened the front flap and pulled out a small, flat purse that contained her passport, credit cards, and some Australian cash. The money was plastic and would be perfectly usable once it dried out; the passport she was a little more concerned about, but it was worth trying to dry it out. The stamps and work visa were still readable, at least.

"Well, at least it'll be easier to get a replacement for a wrecked one than replace a lost one," Rosie said positively, and Olivia cast her a grateful look. "Plus, you've got about a thousand dollars there! I'd have dived into the harbor for that alone."

"Tell me you didn't drop your bag into the harbor and dive in after it," a laughing voice said behind them, and Olivia turned to see that Jill and her busload of guests had arrived.

"Nah, she got one of her snazzy heels caught in the ramp and took a header," Cory said, and it was more than evident that Jill wanted to fall about laughing as she pressed her lips together, eyes glinting with mirth. Instead, she shook her head and turned back to escorting the guests aboard. *They* all got a guiding hand from Jill or the man who'd arrived with her, Olivia noticed a bit jealously. Letting a paying guest fall in the harbor would be bad for business, after all.

A light tug at her wrist made her turn back to Rosie. "It's a half-hour trip to the island. You'll be way more comfortable in dry clothes." Rosie pointed at her suitcase. "There's only a tiny bathroom, but at least you can change."

Grateful for the suggestion, Olivia nodded. She and Rosie retreated to the rear corner of the boat's main cabin while Cory and the other man pulled in the ramp and cast off the lines. Someone else must be upstairs driving the boat, Olivia surmised as huge engines started up and they slid away from the dock.

Another reason to be glad she'd decided to retrieve her bag, Olivia thought as she dug out the key for her luggage lock and opened her suitcase. She had a sinking feeling in the pit of her stomach that absolutely everything she'd brought with her was far too glamorous. Though this was a five-star, premium resort, even the guests were more casually dressed than the most casual outfit she owned.

"Wow," Rosie breathed in astonishment, staring into the case as Olivia took a couple of things off the top layer and set them aside. "You have *really* nice clothes."

"Nobody in New York takes you seriously if you're not wearing a designer label," Olivia said with perfect honesty. "I feel like I'm going to be very overdressed, though." She looked at Rosie's cotton shorts, tank top, and rubber flip-flops. "I don't even *own* a pair of shoes without high heels."

That made Rosie laugh. "You'll be better off barefoot! Almost all the paths on the island are sand; you'd sink in." Lightly fingering the hem of a silk Mossimo dress, she said tentatively, "I have several spare pairs of thongs, and lots of casual gear. We're about the same size. You're welcome to borrow anything you like... if I could maybe borrow one of these gorgeous dresses to wear to the staff Christmas party?"

The Mossimo dress probably cost more than Rosie's entire wardrobe, Olivia knew, but the friendly overture was too kind to ignore. "You're on. But what are thongs? Because I don't think you mean what I understand by thongs...."

Rosie laughed and explained that *thongs* was Australian for *flip-flops*, as Olivia picked out the least dressy thing she could find, a Roberto Cavalli printed jersey dress. At least she had one pair of heels that weren't stilettos, she thought with relief as she dug out her favorite cream linen wedges. *Thank you, Kate Middleton, for making these a fashion statement.*

There was nothing really to be done for her hair; she looked like a drowned rat and there were only paper towels to be found in the tiny bathroom. She washed her face and twisted her hair up into a wet knot atop her head; that would have to do. The light was too poor—and she had too little time—to do a lot about her makeup, but at least she could get rid of the raccoon-like circles under her eyes from her running eyeliner.

"Wow," Rosie breathed as Olivia returned a few minutes later. "How did you do that? You look like a million bucks again!"

Olivia smiled, warmed by the other girl's open friendliness and kind words. "Thanks, Rosie. I was feeling a bit like the Swamp Thing."

"Maybe the Creature from The Black Lagoon?" Cody sniped as he walked past. Rosie whacked at his legs, and he evaded her hand with a laugh. Olivia glared at his retreating back. The guy might be gorgeous, but what an asshole!

"Don't mind Cody, he's a total troll," Rosie said, rolling her eyes.

"I think you're being insulting to trolls," Olivia quipped back, and they laughed. Despite the disaster of her unplanned dip in the harbor,

Olivia relaxed. At least she'd have *one* friend at Sunfish Island Resort, she thought as Rosie leaned across her to point out the window and tell her that they were just about to round the southern tip of the island.

Rosie held Olivia back until the guests had all disembarked. The other man took her suitcase with a friendly grin.

"Tell the porter to take it to 6B, please, Jack," Rosie told him.

"Sure thing." He gave Rosie a casual salute. "And welcome to Sunfish, Olivia."

At least everyone was very friendly, Olivia mused as she followed Rosie, who trailed after the last of the guests. Cory stood by the ramp, offering his hand to her in an exaggerated gesture, his blue eyes glinting with mirth.

She debated giving him a shove into the water. It was a very, very tempting thought... and it was also petty and beneath her. She swallowed the impulse and took his hand, letting him steady her as she crossed the ramp.

"Thanks," she muttered grudgingly.

"You're welcome. And... I'm sorry I wasn't there to help you before."

Startled, her gaze flew up to meet his. He looked quite sincere, and his hand was warm and strong as he held on to her for just a moment longer than necessary.

"Olivia Stratten," a voice said, thankfully obviating her need to think of something to say to Cory's unexpected remark. She let go of his hand and turned to see a handsome man in what she guessed was his early forties and actually wearing a business suit, albeit with an open-necked shirt and no tie. "It's good to meet you. I'm Luke Collyer, the resort general manager." He took in her dripping hair with a curious glance but said nothing about it as he offered his hand for a friendly shake.

"It's very nice to meet you, Mr. Collyer." They'd communicated by email after the resort owners had hired her, and his ideas and incisive manner had impressed Olivia.

"Luke, please. We're not formal here at Sunfish."

She smiled in acknowledgment, following him along the shaded dock and into the hotel's main lobby.

"Wow." Olivia's head tipped up. The atrium was amazing, five stories high with a domed glass roof, and live pines growing in gigantic stone pots. Water trickled from stunning fountains and ran underneath shining plate-glass panels in the floor. There were fish in there, she realized, as one swam directly under her foot. It was hard to know where to put her eyes at any given moment.

"Pretty swish, huh?" Luke gave her a knowing smile. "It's very different to how it looked ten years ago, I can tell you. I was working here as assistant hotel manager at the time."

Most of the photographs available online had been of the old resort, so Olivia knew what he meant. She shook her head in wonderment.

"The owners really did spare no expense."

"This whole building is new." Luke gestured upward at the glass dome. "That even has cyclone shutters that can be closed over it. While we're required to evacuate all guests in the event of an oncoming cyclone because the island may be inundated during a storm surge, the upper floors of this building would actually be quite safe even under the most severe conditions."

"Impressive," Olivia said with a nod, wincing as a trickle of cool water ran down her neck from her soaked hair. Luke tilted his head at her curiously.

"Excuse me for asking, but why is your hair wet?"

She sighed and gave him a rueful smile. "I may as well 'fess up; I'm sure it'll be all over the resort within the hour. I fell off the ramp when boarding the boat."

"You *what?*" Luke looked startled.

"Entirely my own fault, I'm afraid. I was wearing spike heels and not looking where I was going." Luke was clearly making an effort to hold back his laughter. Olivia smiled at him cheekily. "Go on, you might as well laugh. *I've* seen the funny side now, anyway."

He permitted himself a few chortles before shaking his head. "I wish I'd seen it, though I'm sure you're glad I didn't. Well. I was going to ask if you wanted the full tour, but all things considered, I think maybe we'll postpone it to tomorrow morning and let you get settled in today instead. I've got meetings this afternoon, I'm afraid."

She smiled at him gratefully. "I admit I'm eager to get to work... but I'm even more eager to have a proper shower and wash the ocean out of my hair."

"Then let's make that happen." Luke turned to the left and swiped an access card through a slot beside a door marked STAFF ONLY. A short passageway led them outside and down a narrow path between high hedges. "This leads to the senior staff accommodation," he told her. "The cabins were actually part of the old resort; the owners decided to leave them for staff use when they built the new ones. You're in number six, which is a two-bedroom. You're sharing it with Suzannah, our executive chef; she's very nice but you probably won't see a lot of her. She's a workaholic."

Olivia nodded, looking with pleasure at the rustic timber cabins, set on low stumps, as they came upon then. Each had a small covered veranda at the front with a couple of comfortable-looking sun loungers; a brass number was screwed to the front railing on every cabin. It wasn't long before they arrived at number six, and Luke fished in a pocket to pull out a key and an access card, both of which he handed to her.

"The card gets you into all the staff areas of the resort. These cabins don't have electronic access like the newer ones, so you'll need to hang on to the key. It fits both doors to your room: the one that exits onto the veranda and the one into the living area of the cabin. Don't forget to lock both, and don't leave valuables lying around in the common area, because it's not secured; anyone can walk in."

Olivia nodded in understanding as Luke turned the door handle and opened the main cabin door. "This is lovely," she said in pleased surprise, looking around the simply furnished room. It had a tiny kitchenette at the other end, a large squashy couch facing a decent-sized flat-screen TV, and a small dining table with four chairs. The floor was tiled, and everything was immaculately clean.

"Maid service will go over the room once a week, on whatever is Housekeeping's quietest day that week. They can do your room and bathroom if you wish, but you need to let them in." Luke gestured to the door on the right-hand wall. "That's your room."

Her suitcase was already sitting by the door, Olivia noted. "Thanks," she said gratefully.

"I'll leave you to it. Suze will be in the middle of lunch prep, so you won't meet her until this afternoon. I'll get someone to come by and show you around a little bit, take you to the staff dining area—all your meals are included, of course."

"Of course," she echoed with a small smile. She'd never had an all-inclusive *job* before, but then you couldn't actually pay for much on Sunfish apart from drinks, she recalled from reading the existing marketing literature. Feeding the staff was pretty much required when they couldn't easily source their own supplies.

"I'll see you later. Get settled in," Luke left her with a friendly nod. Olivia sighed a little in relief as she was finally left alone, and the tension dropped from her shoulders.

The day had been a mess right from the moment her cab driver in Sydney got a flat tire on the way to the airport and she'd nearly missed her flight. Rising tension and nerves about making a good impression had twisted a tight knot in her stomach, making her unable to eat or drink anything. Feeling an intense thirst, she crossed to the kitchenette to take a look in the fridge. She found several cans of soda, some of brands she didn't recognize. They had to belong to the unknown roommate. Biting her lip, Olivia eventually shrugged and grabbed a cola. She could always replace it later.

Sipping on her purloined cola, she let herself into her room and dragged her suitcase in after her. The bedroom was just as pleasantly furnished as the shared living area, with a double bed, dressing table with large mirror, and to her surprised pleasure, a high-quality desk and office chair with a new-looking computer on the desk. It also had a generous-sized walk-in closet and a beautifully appointed ensuite bathroom.

Delighted by her new living quarters, Olivia decided everything else could wait until she'd showered. The drapes over the sliding door to the veranda were already closed, so she closed her door, stripped, and headed for the ensuite.

CHAPTER THREE

Half an hour later, Olivia felt a good deal more human. She'd showered and washed her hair, put on the fluffy bathrobe she'd found hanging on the back of the bathroom door, and was now sorting through her suitcase rather despairingly, wondering what on earth she could wear. Everything she'd brought now looked far too formal, even though she'd selected the most "casual" items from her wardrobe before putting everything into storage back in New York.

A light tap on the door leading out to the veranda made her look up. She could only make out a vague shape through the sheer curtain. "Who is it?" she called.

"Rosie!"

Smiling, Olivia went to let her new friend in, her smile widening even further as she saw the armload of clothes Rosie was carrying. "Oh, you star. I was just wondering what to wear in order not to look completely overdressed."

Rosie smiled shyly back at her, piling the clothes on the bed. "I think you look great. Your clothes are just gorgeous."

"They are," Olivia agreed, "and they're perfect for New York City life, or even Sydney, but here on Sunfish I'll just look... I don't know. Like I think I'm better than everyone else. I want to fit in here, be part of this lovely staff-family vibe you all seem to have going on."

"You will! Everyone's really nice and welcoming. And... well, to be honest, probably falling in the harbor really helped, because now they all know a funny story about you and it'll be a good icebreaker for you to get to know everyone."

Olivia smiled wryly, choosing a pair of shorts and a flowered blouse from the pile Rosie had put down and taking them to the bathroom to dress. "And here I was thinking I'd made a disastrous first impression," she called back.

"Well"—Rosie looked at the laptop and tablet lying on a soggy towel on the desk—"I mean, it was a disaster in some ways, but in others it could be a blessing in disguise?" She looked up at Olivia as she returned from the bathroom.

"I've seen the funny side now, anyway." Olivia grinned back at her. "When Luke said he wished he'd seen it, I got a mind's-eye picture of how I must have looked and almost cracked up laughing on the spot."

"That's the spirit," Rosie said warmly. She took a pair of pink rubber flip-flops—*thongs*, Olivia remembered, sternly telling herself not to snicker—from the pile of clothes and held them out. "These ones are fairly new. Should last you awhile."

"I'm only borrowing these until I have a chance to go back over to Hamilton Island and go shopping," Olivia told her, accepting the shoes.

"Oh, don't. Everything there is really expensive because it's all brought in for tourists. Take the other boat over to Airlie Beach on the mainland—that one goes every day too. The supermarket is only a five-minute walk from the marina, and there are plenty of other shops too."

"That's good to know, thanks!" Olivia made a mental note to ask Luke which day she could do that. "And how about doing laundry?"

"I'll show you where the staff laundry is on the way to lunch. You ready?"

Olivia scooped her keys and access card off the desk. "I am now."

As they left the cabin, Rosie pointed to their right, away from the main resort building. "I'm in the next cabin, by the way, number 7. Jill and I share it. Suze, your roomie, is a close friend; she often comes over and hangs out with us. You're welcome too, anytime."

Olivia nodded. "Thank you," she said genuinely.

They girls turned to walk back toward the main resort, and a deep voice stopped them in their tracks.

"Well, well, it's the Little Mermaid! How's tricks, Ariel?"

Cory leaned on the veranda rail of the cabin next to her own, a broad grin on his face. Remembering the way he'd apologized to her as she left the boat, and thinking of Rosie's advice to look at the whole incident as a blessing in disguise, Olivia flipped him the bird with an answering grin. Cory laughed, vaulted easily over the rail, and fell into step beside them.

"Good to see you can laugh about it." He smiled down at Olivia. She had to fight not to be knocked sideways from the impact of his good looks again; that combined with an intoxicating, spicily masculine scent as he stood close to her made her head reel.

"I can laugh about it, but call me Ariel again and *you* won't be laughing," she said in a mock-menacing tone, narrowing her eyes at him.

Cory laughed again and nodded amiably.

Stop being nice, you're making it very hard for me to keep my mind out of your pants, Olivia thought with an internal sigh, and resolutely turned her eyes away from his chiseled, handsome features. She caught Rosie giving her a speculative look and did her best to smooth her face to neutrality.

"Cory's single, y'know," Rosie murmured as they stood in line for the lunch buffet in the staff dining room. Cory had peeled off to go speak to someone else and was thankfully out of earshot.

"Oh?" Olivia tried to keep her tone light and disinterested. "Why?" she had to ask. "I mean..."

"I know, and trust me, it's not like he doesn't get offers." Rosie gave her a conspiratorial grin. "Every week there's a few tourists trying to throw themselves at him, but Cory's not the sort to have flings." She handed Olivia a plate. "I've known him forever. We were in school together in Cairns as kids."

That explained how comfortable the pair of them seemed; they really were childhood friends. Olivia did her best to divert the subject, though. "You grew up in Cairns, so you're a North Queenslander?"

"Spent my whole life on or near the Reef," Rosie confirmed. "I'd never want to be anywhere else."

"Hear, hear," Cory affirmed, rejoining them and collecting his own plate. "It's 'beautiful one day, perfect the next,' don't y'know." He quoted the Queensland advertising slogan at Olivia.

"I haven't been here long enough to confirm the truth of that," she pointed out, "but I'm looking forward to finding out."

"You'll see." Cory sounded utterly confident. Looking at both him and Rosie, incredibly healthy-looking, tanned, and practically glowing compared to her pasty-pale self, Olivia could quite believe it. "Although you'll need to use some pretty heavy-duty sunblock," Cory continued, "or that lovely creamy skin will be lobster-red."

"I bought a bottle in Sydney," Olivia agreed, "and I'll get more when I go into Airlie Beach to shop Rosie's been kind enough to lend me a few things, but I'll need to make a trip."

"Thought I recognized that blouse." Cory grinned at Rosie as the three of them left the buffet and headed over to a table. "Looks better on Olivia, I'm afraid."

Rosie made a face at him, but she also gave Olivia a sideways glance and a surreptitious nudge in the ribs. Olivia rolled her eyes in return.

"We are not thirteen," she hissed in Rosie's ear as another man paused by their table, distracting Cory briefly. "Stop trying to matchmake!"

Rosie laughed but turned her attention to her food, which was well worth paying attention to, Olivia conceded. The buffet had a huge variety, everything beautifully presented and perfectly fresh. She scooped up a forkful of pasta salad and hummed with pleasure at the taste.

The other man who'd stopped to speak to Cory took the fourth seat at their table then, and Olivia swallowed hastily as Cory introduced him.

"Olivia, this is Bryce, the resort's dive master. Bryce, meet Olivia."

Bryce was younger than the other two; Olivia estimated him to be about twenty-three or twenty-four. His dark hair was buzzed close to his scalp, and his deep bronze tan set off grass-green eyes.

Involuntarily, Olivia wondered whether all Australian men were this attractive. Cory, Luke, and Bryce, the three she'd met on Sunfish Island so far, were all good-looking enough to be models... though if she were completely honest,

Cory was the only one who'd sparked more in her than a mere aesthetic appreciation. She smiled at Bryce's cheerful greeting.

"Nice to meet you too."

"So when are you coming out for your first dive with me?" Bryce asked. Olivia blinked, another forkful of food on her way to her mouth.

"Uh, what?"

"No way can you effectively market this place without seeing its primary attraction. The Reef. And you can't really see the Reef without diving on it."

"Technically she already made her first dive," Cory said, grinning, and Olivia had absolutely no compunctions about kicking him in the shin under the table.

Bryce frowned with confusion, and Olivia realized that news of her plunge hadn't reached him yet. Prudently moving his shins out of her reach, Cory promptly filled Bryce in. Olivia settled for glaring at him, though the way Cory described her had her inwardly glowing. Or maybe not so inwardly, considering the way Rosie was smirking at her.

"You should have seen her. She dived off the boat like an Olympic champion," Cory concluded. "I half expected her to turn a double somersault on the way in. I'd give her a 9.9 for execution. She sure was a sight for sore eyes coming out too."

A little puzzled at that remark, Olivia frowned at him; at least until Rosie murmured in her ear, "Your blouse went transparent. Cory got quite the eyeful."

Olivia hoped the two men interpreted her flaming cheeks as being caused by Bryce's laughter. Picking up her water glass, she took a deep gulp. "I daresay people will be telling stories of my arrival for years," she said, "getting more exaggerated with each telling."

"It's a good enough story that we don't need to exaggerate." Cory grinned at her. She considered the position of his shins with a tilt of her head, making him chuckle. She picked a cherry tomato off her plate and flung it with deadly accuracy at his forehead instead.

"Now, now, children." Bryce caught the tomato as it bounced off Cory's skull, "settle down. You've got to work together."

"Quite," Olivia said. "You've had your fun at my expense," she told Cory directly. "Now can you just let it go—at least when I'm in earshot?"

"Fair enough." He shrugged amiably. "God knows I make an idiot of myself regularly enough that you'll soon have plenty of ammunition for return fire, anyway."

"I can certainly attest to that," Rosie agreed. "I have a million embarrassing stories about him from our schooldays I can share if he keeps being obnoxious, anyway."

Cory's blue eyes widened comically. "I'll behave," he said hurriedly.

Olivia had to laugh at his schoolboyish dismay. "You better." She pointed her fork at him.

"Yes, ma'am." He saluted her smartly. She didn't miss the warmth in his eyes as he looked back at her; a matching heat bloomed low in her belly. Pressing her knees together, Olivia looked away from those mesmerizing blue eyes and prodded at her lunch with her fork. Strangely enough, she no longer felt hungry.

Bryce and Rosie mercifully started talking, filling in the silence, and Olivia was content to just listen to their chatter. She glanced up at Cory through her lashes and found him pushing his food around his plate as well. He seemed to sense her eyes on him and looked up at her.

Their gazes caught and held.

She half expected him to make a quip or some sarcastic remark, but he just stared back at her, holding the fork still in his hand. For an endless moment they stared at each other, oblivious to the chatter and noise around them.

This is a terrible idea, Olivia thought. *I have to work with him.*

Cory smiled, the expression almost shy.

Oh, fuck it. Terrible idea or not, I'm not going to live like a nun for the next twelve months.

She smiled back.

Shortly afterwards, Rosie said apologetically that she had work to do, and Bryce left to take a new-divers class in one of the resort pools. They headed off leaving Olivia and Cory still staring at each other over the remains of their lunch.

"Do you have somewhere you need to be?" Olivia asked finally.

"Not until four thirty. Um. Luke actually asked me if I'd show you around a bit, but... if you'd rather someone else, I'm sure I can rustle someone up."

Time to make the call, Olivia.

"I wouldn't rather anyone else."

Cory's smile was slow and sure, warming through her. "Good," he said softly. "That's good. C'mon, then."

He offered a hand as she stood. Olivia debated taking it and decided she'd given the resort staff enough gossip for her first day. Besides, if she stepped a little closer, she could thread her hand through his arm instead and rest it on the pleasing bulge of his biceps. She got a few interested looks as she made her way out of the dining room on Cory's arm.

A row of golf buggies was parked behind the resort. Cory handed her into the passenger seat of one before going around to the driver's side.

"Please tell me that you don't drive like Rosie," Olivia thought to say suddenly, grabbing the dash as Cory started the engine.

He burst out laughing. "I promise I don't drive like Rosie. She's a maniac. Never has passed her driver's test; she can't drive anywhere except here or on Hamilton, with the golf buggies... and she's banned from driving one here too."

"That's a relief." Olivia took her hands off the dash before saying tentatively, "I've never learned to drive. It wasn't really necessary living in New York. The subway goes everywhere. Maybe you could teach me?"

"Sure," he said cheerfully, "want to start now?"

She laughed. "No, let me figure out my way around from the passenger seat first. I don't think I can concentrate on trying to drive while gaping like the tourist I am."

"Gotcha. Well, if you're the tourist, let me play tour guide." Cory slowed the golf cart as the path they were on intersected with another; he looked left and right before turning left. "First thing to note for when you do start driving: all our paths here are two-way and we drive on the *left* here in Oz."

"Noted," she agreed. "What's that?" She pointed off to the left at a small white building standing alone on a small rise.

"One of the wedding chapels. We have three, and an average of just under two weddings a day here. We have facilities for a lot more, and that's part of what Luke wants you to push in the marketing, I know... that this is one of the best wedding destinations in Australia."

"I can see why," Olivia agreed as Cory pulled the buggy off the path into a small parking area near the chapel. They got out and walked up to the small building. On closer inspection, she could see it was open on three sides, facing out over a small palm-fringed cove. The white sand and blue water were a stunning backdrop.

"Wow," she breathed, taking in the surroundings. "Just wow."

"Yeah." Cory placed his hands on the low railing at the side of the chapel, looking out over the water. "I see this view every day and I never get tired of it."

"I can imagine." Leaning into the railing as she stood beside him, Olivia gazed out at the ocean in wonder, taking in the colors in the water as the depth changed. "I've never seen anything like it. So many colors!"

"Beautiful," Cory agreed, but he was looking down at her now, not out at the water. Lifting one hand from the railing, he gently brushed a strand of curly, brown hair back behind her ear. "I was knocked sideways when I saw you walking down the dock today, Olivia," he said quietly, "and I feel like maybe you feel the same way, a bit."

She turned big dark brown eyes up to his but said nothing. He plowed on stubbornly. "Physical attraction is one thing, and I could put it to one side easily enough, but... everything about you has hit me for six. The way you dived back in to find your passport; the way you put me in my place for laughing at you. This might be crazy because we have to work together, but I'm seriously attracted to you. And I'd like to make that clear now, before we even get started. I don't want there to be any misunderstandings. If you're not interested, or if you want me to keep my distance because we're work colleagues, I can respect that, but I need you to set a boundary here. Because I don't want there to be *any* boundaries. I feel like you've been giving me some signals, but I need to make sure I'm not misinterpreting you."

He was being incredibly honest and direct, laying his soul bare to her with the heartfelt words. Olivia took a deep breath. "I think I might feel the same way. Except... what does 'hit for six' mean?"

Cory's serious expression dissolved and he let out a hearty chuckle. "It's a cricket term. Like... hitting a home run in baseball."

"You do know that hitting a home run has another meaning altogether, right?"

"I know." Slowly, giving her plenty of time to pull away, he put one arm around her, settling it lightly on her waist. "We can take this as slow or as fast as you like, Olivia."

She looked up at him and smiled coquettishly, turning to face him fully and lifting her hands to set them on his shoulders. "Slow's never been my style."

"I'm really glad you said that," Cory murmured, arm tightening around her to draw her close. He sank his free hand into her curly hair to hold her head still as he bent to kiss her.

Cory's mouth was hot and sweet-tasting as it moved over hers; gentle at first, at least until Olivia nipped his bottom lip. He let out a little growl at that and deepened the kiss, tongue sliding into her mouth possessively. She slid her fingers into his blond hair and gripped, nails scraping at his scalp, going up on tiptoe to push her body firmly against his, crush her breasts against the hardness of his chest.

They were both breathing raggedly when the kiss finally ended. Cory's hand shook as he brushed his knuckles over Olivia's cheek and traced a fingertip over her kiss-swollen lips.

Neither of them spoke; words would have ruined the moment, and they knew each other too little as yet to really know what to say. Instead Cory dropped his hand from Olivia's face reluctantly as she took a step back. He smiled as she slipped her hand into his.

"Why don't you give me the rest of the tour?"

CHAPTER FOUR

Sunfish Island was bigger than Olivia had realized. She'd studied the official literature, of course, and looked at photos and maps on the internet, but there so much of it had to be seen in person to be appreciated. Every turn in the path seemed to bring a new stunning view, another delightful residence or grouping of cabins.

"This place is just incredible," she said as Cory drove them into another part of the resort, where he pulled up within sight of a sparkling lagoon pool fringed with palm trees. "Just... I mean, I knew it was beautiful from the photos, but photos just don't do it justice."

"That's where you come in." Cory hopped out of the golf cart and gestured her to follow as he headed over to the thatched-roof bar beside the pool. "I personally think we need TV advertising. Sunfish Island had a reputation here in Australia as a cheap family place to go, back in the nineties and early two thousands. There's almost nothing now that was even here back then—a cyclone eight years ago put paid to most of the old buildings. The cabins we live in are among the few survivors."

"I see." Olivia slipped onto a stool beside Cory at the bar and waited as the bartender made drinks for a couple of guests. "So the existing reputation has it marketed to the wrong kind of clientele, because although Sunfish is family-friendly, it's five-star and certainly not cheap these days."

"Exactly. Plus, we need to get known outside of Australia. The Chinese, Japanese, Indian, and Russian tourist market is huge these days, and they're prepared to pay for top quality."

"Hey, Cory." The conversation was interrupted by the bartender, a petite, beautiful young woman with dark brown skin and long braids.

"This is Olivia, Nessa. She's our new marketing manager. Nessa is the best bartender on the island," Cory confided.

"Ahem!"

"Beg your pardon, in Queensland. In Australia! Probably the world!" Cory grinned and Nessa laughed.

"Better. Nice to meet you, Olivia." She leaned across the bar to shake hands.

"You're English," Olivia realized after hearing her accent.

"I certainly am. Been out here ten years and you'd have to drag me away kicking and screaming." She slid a coaster in front of each of them on the polished timber bar. "What can I get you?"

"I'm on duty later, so just a soda water for me, thanks," Cory said cheerfully. "Like a beer, Olivia? Or a cocktail?"

She'd dearly love a cold beer, and said so. Nessa set a bottle beaded with condensation on the counter beside a clean glass.

"One of our local lagers, give it a try."

One sip told Olivia that Nessa had made the right call; she took a long draught to soak the parched feeling in her throat and sighed with pleasure. "Lovely. Thank you."

"Welcome." Nessa gave her a bright smile and darted away to serve another customer who approached the bar, her long braids swinging.

"What's the policy regarding staff using the resort facilities?" Olivia asked as Cory take a long drink of his soda water, his throat working as he swallowed.

"Perfectly fine as long as you don't drink alcohol while you're working, are never inebriated on resort premises, and don't prevent a customer from using the facility. So if it's busy, find somewhere else to go, basically." Cory shrugged. "The resort is overstaffed and underoccupied at the moment, so it shouldn't be an issue." He lowered his voice. "We don't pay for soft drinks 'on tap' and you pay only cost price on other drinks, so it's a really good deal. We're very well looked after here." He nodded towards Nessa, who was expertly making a cocktail. "I prefer this bar because Nessa runs tabs for all of us on sight—she's much more relaxed about it than the other bartenders. Plus, it's only a five-minute walk from the staff accommodation."

"It is?" Olivia blinked, looking around. She'd gotten completely turned around on the tour, then. She could have sworn they were a long way from the main resort, but looking around now, she could just see the dome of the main building above the palm trees. "Oh, I see."

"I'll show you the path later. This is the closest swimming pool to the cabins too, and you can also swim at the beach down there." Cory pointed.

"It's safe?"

"Beach swimming? Yes, it's really shallow up to about a hundred meters out, and this isn't stinger season. No sharks, either. You should wear reef shoes, though, because there can be sharp coral and stonefish, which you do *not* want to step on."

"Venomous?"

"Yes. Spines on their backs. The pain is hideous, I'm told." Cory shuddered. "We've never had anyone stung here, but that doesn't mean you shouldn't be careful."

"I shall consider myself properly cautioned." Olivia smiled at him. "I did read up on Australia's wildlife before I accepted the job."

"And you weren't put off? Brave girl."

They both chuckled.

"Tell me about you, Olivia. I know enough about Hunter Enterprises to know the bosses would have hired the best. So why was the best willing to give up what was clearly a very lucrative and respected position in New York and fly halfway around the world to spend a year here? Because love this place though I do, it has to feel like the back of beyond to a sophisticated city girl like you."

His blue eyes were clear and calm as he watched her. Olivia took a deep breath, puffed her cheeks on the way out, and took another long sip of her beer.

"You're not starting with the easy questions, are you?" She smiled to take the sting from her words. "I guess we should start this off being honest with each other, though." Another long sip of beer, and she looked away from his clear blue eyes, which seemed to see right into her soul. "I *had* to get out."

He only listened, doing his best to be quiet and really pay attention to not just her words, but the emotions behind them, as she continued.

"I'd been in the rat race since my teens, since my parents enrolled me in an exclusive Manhattan prep school. There was this intense pressure to be the best, the smartest, the most popular. Some girls couldn't handle it; they cracked, took drugs, slept around. I thrived on it." Twirling her beer bottle in her fingers, she said, "I was always top of the pile. I was the one who got the internships, the scholarships, won the awards. Everything came so easily. Got picked up straight out of Stanford Business School to work at the top marketing firm in New York, made associate in two years, became the youngest partner in the firm's history on my twenty-sixth birthday."

Cory said nothing, just watched as Olivia talked. Her voice had no real pride in it as she talked about her achievements; she might have been reciting a grocery list for all the emotion she showed. Her eyes flicked back to his. "And with all the success came money, more of it than I really knew what to do with... and the perfect partner to share it all with."

He'd wondered if that would come up. There was no way a woman as beautiful and successful as Olivia hadn't had men falling at her feet.

"Brad Cochrane. Or as my friends dubbed him after the breakup, The Cockroach." She gave him a little half smile. "One of Wall Street's finest."

"Wait a minute," Cory suddenly put two and two together. "I know that name. Isn't he that guy who was recently convicted in the biggest money-laundering case in history? For the Mexican drug cartels?"

"Bingo." Olivia made finger guns and pointed them at him. "As his fiancée, I was suspect number two. Took me months to clear my name. Most of my assets are still sequestered, and almost all of my legitimate clients suddenly really wanted to work with other partners at the firm. I was asked to take a leave of absence... and then the contents of my desk got delivered to my apartment in a UPS box."

"Jeez, Olivia, that must have been absolute hell," Cory said quietly. He couldn't even imagine what she'd gone through, her professional reputation ruined by something that had absolutely nothing to do with her at the same time as her relationship collapsed under a tissue of lies. "I'm so sorry."

She drained the last of her beer and set the glass down on the bar. "I sued for wrongful dismissal... and lost. There was a clause in my contract about not bringing my good name into disrepute, and my name had been smeared all over the news in connection with Brad's. Even though I had nothing to do with his shit, I still lost everything. My job, my reputation... and after the lawsuit, there was no way any firm in New York would ever hire me again. All because I had the shitty taste to fall for a con artist."

There was really nothing Cory could say. What had happened to Olivia was deeply unfair. She gave him a wan little smile.

"So you see, I really didn't have all that many options when John Hunter called me. I'd just pitched a marketing campaign for his California winery when all the shit went down. He liked it, called to take me up on it, and was seriously unhappy when he found out I wouldn't be able to handle the campaign after all. He asked me to handle it privately, which I did... I had no idea when or if I'd ever get another job at all, and the lawsuit had eaten most of my savings. The launch went off really well despite everything, and he offered me this job. The rest, as they say, is history."

She shrugged, looking away at the ocean again. "You know, I don't regret it. It was killing me slowly, the constant pressure to dress the part, be seen in all the right places, be friends with all the right people. This"—she swept a hand around, indicating their peaceful surroundings— "maybe here I can find out who Olivia Stratten actually is when she's not under pressure to be perfect."

Cory bit his lip on the remark that almost spilled from him. Olivia turned to him, her eyes dancing with mirth.

"Maybe that's why I feel so comfortable with you already. You definitely don't know Perfect Olivia."

"I wasn't gonna say it." His grin broke out, though. "You did look like perfection walking down the dock. I was very intimidated."

"Until my clumsy ass fell in the harbor." She snickered, eyes alight.

On impulse he took her hand. "Olivia Stratten is someone who can laugh at herself, and that's the first trait I look for in a woman: a good sense of humor."

Laughing freely at that, Olivia squeezed his hand back. "Well. A couple of months ago, I'm pretty sure I wouldn't have seen the funny side, but I definitely do now."

Cory looked at his watch then and said with regret that he needed to get back. They waved to Nessa, who was just getting busy with the early evening cocktail hour, and hopped back in the golf cart. He pointed out the walking path, which was a shortcut to the cabins as they passed it.

"I have to go call the early evening bingo game," Cory said regretfully. "It's our regular bingo caller's day off."

Olivia laughed at the thought of Cory calling bingo numbers to a crowd of retirees. Because he was the activities director, she supposed he had to be able to cover for any of his team when required, though. Thinking that she needed to know more about the activities and events the resort offered, she questioned him about his job. Cory answered all her questions good-naturedly, clearly happy to talk about the job he obviously adored.

"Bryce was right when he said you really need to see the Reef, though," he said as he pulled the golf buggy back into the parking slot they'd taken it from. "Have you ever dived before?"

She shook her head. "Not proper diving with oxygen tanks, no. I'm a strong swimmer, though."

"That I already knew." He cast her a grin. "Well, you'd have to take a couple of Bryce's starter lessons in the pool to begin with, but I'm taking a group out snorkeling tomorrow, if you'd be interested?"

"I'd love to," Olivia said enthusiastically, before she thought to say, "I don't know if Luke will want me to start work here, though..."

"It's an early afternoon tour. You can catch up with him in the morning and see," Cory suggested. "I'm pretty sure he'll tell you to take a few days and familiarize yourself with everything the resort has to offer before you consider implementing anything, though."

That sounded like a sensible strategy. "Well, provided he's okay with it, yes, I'd love to come snorkeling."

"Excellent. Boat leaves the dock at one; we've got plenty of snorkeling gear, but make sure you bring your own sunscreen." He grinned down at her, and as they approached the door leading back into the main building, he drew her gently to a stop with his hand on her elbow. "There's nothing I'd like more than to spend the whole evening getting to know you, Olivia. I'm sorry I can't."

Cory's eyes were serious as he looked down at her. She smiled back at him, charmed again by his honesty and his straightforward, open approach.

"I'd like that too."

"I'm honored by your trust in telling me about your ex and why you're here, and I promise you that nobody will hear a word of it from me."

She was already quite sure of that, but she nodded anyway, accepting his pledge. Cory bent his head slowly, allowing her time to move away if she wanted to, but she was more than happy to step in closer and accept the kiss he pressed against her lips.

"Tomorrow," he said, a low-voiced promise, before he swiped his access card and let them back into the building.

Olivia was sure the color flags were flying high on her cheeks as she watched Cory bound up the spiral stairs in the atrium to the main lounge on the second floor where he had to call the bingo game. She caught herself admiring at the muscles bunching in his strong thighs as he took the steps three at a time, and laughed at herself. Cory was a whole lot more than just a handsome face and an attractive body.

"He's good-looking for sure, but Cory's a player," a voice said behind her, and Olivia turned to see Jill, the guest relations manager she'd met at the airport. "Don't get your heart broken."

Olivia wasn't entirely sure what made her ask, "Is that personal experience talking?" but the way Jill's face flushed told her that her shot in the dark was right on target. Jill didn't say another word, just turned and stalked away, outrage radiating from her in waves.

"I think I might have made an enemy," Olivia muttered regretfully. She couldn't do a lot about it, though; she guessed that the moment Jill so much as suspected chemistry between Olivia and Cory, her nose would have been out of joint. Thank God nobody had witnessed their kiss at the wedding chapel, or the quick embrace outside the door. Olivia's name would have been mud all over Sunfish Island before nightfall; no doubt she'd have been smeared as a slut who threw herself at Cory literally as soon as she arrived.

Wandering over to look at the tour-booking desk—currently unoccupied—and the large display of brochures for available trips, Olivia wondered if she *had* been slutty. She'd always had a policy of never getting involved with anyone she worked with. What was it about Cory that had made her forget that resolution within a couple of hours of meeting him? It wasn't just the way he looked. She'd worked with attractive men many times before and never felt remotely tempted. No, she felt a genuine connection with Cory, one that had been there from their first meeting, and every moment spent in his company since had only reinforced the impression that he was a man she could like and respect as well as lust after.

I'm not going to feel guilty for going after what I want, Olivia decided, squaring her shoulders and turning to look around the lobby. Whatever had happened between Jill and Cory was obviously in the past, and Jill's little display of jealousy only put Olivia on her guard. She couldn't trust anything Jill said about Cory now. Every instinct told her that Cory wasn't a "player" as Jill had described him—and wouldn't Rosie, who'd known Cory all her life, have dropped a gentle hint or two if he were, instead of eagerly matchmaking?

CHAPTER FIVE

Just as Olivia thought of Rosie, she came through a door on the other side of the lobby with Luke, the pair of them talking earnestly. They both spotted her and smiled at the same moment, coming over to join her.

"Hey, how are you settling in?" Luke asked cheerfully. "Better after the dunking?" His eyes twinkled.

"Much, thank you," Olivia said. "Rosie was kind enough to lend me some of her things, I'm afraid I vastly overestimated the dress code here at Sunfish. I think I'll need to go into Airlie Beach to shop one day, if that can be arranged?"

"Of course, the boat goes every day," Luke said with a shrug. "You can go anytime you like. As far as I'm concerned, you make your own schedule here, Olivia. The only instruction I have from Mr. Hunter is that I'm to see to it you have anything you need. Rosie mentioned your laptop and tablet took a dunking too."

"And my phone," she admitted. "Yes, I'll need to purchase replacements for those in Airlie as well."

"The resort has an account at the computer-and-electrical store. Put them on our tab." Luke's tone brooked no argument.

"Well... thank you," she accepted gracefully, secretly grateful. Replacing her electronics would have put a serious dent in her much-depleted savings. "That's very good of you."

He waved away her thanks. "There's a computer in your room, too, but that's mainly because I don't really have office space for you. You're welcome to work anywhere you like in the resort. Although you're on staff, you're not part of the guest relations side, and as such I don't mind if you want to act more as a guest here, to get the real guest experience, than as a staff member."

Startled, Olivia blinked at him. "Thank you! But I want to pull my weight around here too. If you need an extra pair of hands at any time, please just say so."

"Rosie will let you know." Luke gestured at Rosie, who hadn't said a word as she nodded along in agreement with what he was saying. "She's our staff manager."

"Well, there may be times when we do need extra pairs of hands, of course," Rosie said, "but I'll try not to shove you into anything you wouldn't be prepared for. I mean, I'm guessing you're going to spend a fair bit of time talking to guests anyway, asking them what they think are the best things about Sunfish for marketing purposes, so guest relations would probably be a handy spot for you. Which is Jill's department, of course."

"Of course," Olivia echoed, doing her level best not to let her feelings at the idea of having to work for Jill, even temporarily, show on her face.

She must have failed, though, because after dinner—eaten with Luke and Rosie, who both talked enthusiastically about how much they loved working at Sunfish—she was walking back to her cabin with Rosie when the other girl asked, "Um, Olivia, I hope you don't mind me asking this, but have you had a run-in with Jill?"

She missed a step, recovered. "I thought I wasn't that obvious."

"Jill has a way of rubbing people up the wrong way, sometimes."

"One would think that guest relations wouldn't be the best career for her, then," Olivia said dryly.

"You'd be surprised the shit she has to deal with," Rosie replied. "Guest relations manager is just a fancy title for 'troubleshooter.'"

"Hm." They'd reached her cabin, and Olivia stopped and turned to Rosie with a sigh. "I don't want to get off on the wrong foot, and I don't want to make any enemies, but I'm pretty sure Jill was predisposed to dislike me from the moment Cory started flirting with me."

"She was predisposed to dislike you from the moment she saw you in the airport and realized how pretty you are," Rosie said bluntly. "Because yes, as you've already figured out, Cory is a sore spot with Jill."

"Will you tell me about it?" Olivia pleaded. "I know Jill is your friend and I don't want to ask you to go behind her back, but I'm pretty sure I can't trust anything she says about Cory... and I'm pretty sure I *can* trust what *you* tell me about him, since you've known each other so long."

Rosie sighed and glanced at the lit window in her cabin next door. "Invite me in?"

"Sure."

They went into the lounge area and sat down. Rosie rubbed her hands together, looking as though she was thinking about what to say. Olivia waited in silence, not wanting to push. Jill and Rosie were obviously close, and she didn't want to force Rosie to betray her friend.

"Cory and Jill dated for a while when Jill got the job here in the middle of last year," Rosie said finally. "It lasted, maybe three or four months? I don't remember exactly."

"Why did they break up? I don't need all the gory details," Olivia said hurriedly, "but who dumped who would be good to know."

"Cory ended it, but Jill drove him to it. She was incredibly clingy and possessive. I'm sure you can imagine that with the way Cory looks, he literally can't help girls throwing themselves at him sometimes. There was this guest at the resort. She was here with her parents; she wouldn't leave him alone. She was all of seventeen, so Cory just treated her like a kid with a crush... which was exactly the right thing to do. He was polite but didn't encourage her, and he made damn sure she couldn't catch him alone anywhere. Which didn't stop Jill from getting wildly jealous every time Cory even glanced in her direction." Rosie sighed and leaned back in her chair. "Jill was being stupid, I told her so myself; told her Cory would never touch the girl."

"But she wouldn't listen," Olivia surmised.

"Yup, and in the end there was a really ugly scene where Jill confronted the girl and called her all sorts of demeaning names, told her to stay away from Cory. Honestly I think the only reason Jill didn't get fired for it was that the parents thought their daughter had been making a fool of herself and took *Jill's* side when the matter went up before Luke."

Olivia shook her head. "That... must have been pretty hard on the girl."

"Which was what Cory thought. The whole scene was just so unnecessary, and he told Jill that when he broke it off. She'd been jealous over nothing and he could see it inevitably happening again, every time he even so much as spoke to a pretty girl. He didn't want the drama."

And here I come with a history of nothing but *drama*, Olivia thought. "Thanks for telling me this, Rosie."

"You're welcome. I'd like to see Cory happy. I'd like to see Jill happy too, but the two of them just aren't suited for each other." Rosie shrugged, her irrepressible grin breaking out again. "I'm a natural matchmaker."

"What about you, anyone special in your life?" Olivia asked curiously.

A wistful look crossed Rosie's face briefly before she shook her head. "I'm afraid not."

"That look tells me that there's someone, though? Didn't Jill say you were seeing a pilot?"

Olivia remembered the earlier conversation in the airport.

"Past tense, I'm afraid."

"I'm sorry to hear that," Olivia said genuinely.

"He was seeing multiple other girls"—Rosie's smile was wry—"and nice though he was—and honest about it, which was a big point in his favor—I'd like to be somebody's one and only."

Don't we all, Olivia thought. "Jill told me Cory was a player."

"Not in the least." Rosie shook her head vehemently. "Couldn't be further from the truth. Cory isn't one to start something unless he thinks it's going somewhere. He was genuinely broken up about ending things with Jill, but her jealousy was just too much for the relationship to bear."

"So me even hinting that I might be jealous would be a big red flag," Olivia surmised. "I'll keep that in mind."

"You should. Because there are silly young girls who try to throw themselves at him every other week here, and Cory will be watching to see your reaction," Rosie warned. She covered a huge yawn and laughed at herself. "God, sorry. Been a long day. I'm gonna go crash."

"Thank you for telling me the truth."

"You're welcome." Rosie surprised Olivia with a hug, which Olivia returned tentatively. "Don't let Jill get to you. If I see or hear her starting any crap, I'll try and pull her up; she listens to me."

Olivia thanked her again, and Rosie took her leave with a cheerful wave, leaving Olivia alone with her thoughts.

Lost in thought, Olivia sat for a while in silence. She was startled when the cabin door opened and looked up to see a tall redheaded woman who was probably a couple of years her senior entering.

"Hi," she said uncertainly.

"'Allo, you must be Olivia! I have heard so much about you already! I'm Suzannah, your roommate."

"Oh." Getting to her feet, Olivia smiled in welcome. "Hi—nobody mentioned you were French!"

Suzannah laughed throatily, stepping forward and kissing Olivia enthusiastically on both cheeks. "Eh, we are a multinational crew here; nobody thinks much of it. As long as they can understand your accent, that is."

That made Olivia smile. She liked Suzannah immediately, admiring her poise and confident air. "I swiped one of your sodas from the fridge earlier," she confessed, figuring she'd best get that out of the way first. "I'll replace it, I promise."

Suzannah waved it off with another laugh, heading to the fridge herself. "Want another? I'm thirsty, been a busy night in the kitchen."

Olivia accepted the offer and they sat to introduce themselves to each other properly. Suzannah was more than happy to answer questions, talking about her training at Le Cordon Bleu in Paris and her past work in major hotels and famous restaurants. Olivia almost died of shock when Suzannah admitted to once having worked for Gordon Ramsey and having a glowing recommendation from the infamously critical chef on her résumé.

"Well, nothing I've ever done compares to that; you definitely win," Olivia said, very impressed, making Suzannah's throaty laugh ring out again. The French girl smothered a yawn then, admitting that she'd had a long day.

"Go sleep, we can talk more tomorrow. We've got plenty of time to get to know each other," Olivia insisted when Suzannah demurred, offering to keep her company. Left alone, she thought she should probably go on into her own room, in case she made noise in the lounge area and kept the weary chef awake.

At least the nightwear she'd brought was perfectly fine; she liked to be comfortable when she slept, so she just changed into a tank top and a pair of boyleg cotton shorts before slipping into bed and turning out the bedside light.

Sleep was nowhere to be found, though, and after a couple of hours tossing and turning, Olivia gave up. Getting out of bed, she went out onto her little veranda, sitting down on the chair and putting her feet up on the railing. It was blissfully cool outside now, whereas her room had been too warm; she sighed as the sea breeze washed over her and let her head tip back.

"Can't sleep either?" a low voice said, and she startled upright, yelping with shock as her feet fell to the floor.

"Sorry!"

"Who the hell is that?" Olivia pressed her hand to her pounding heart.

"Cory. Remember, I live next door?" There was a laugh in his voice.

"God damn it." She shut her eyes before opening them, laughing at herself and peering across the dark space between the two cabins. She could just about make him out in the dim moonlight, lying in... "Is that a hammock?"

"Sure is, and it's big enough to share. Wanna come join me?"

She hesitated only briefly before scrambling to her feet and heading over. "I've never been in a hammock before," she admitted, looking at Cory sprawled negligently in the net, one long leg hanging over the side. "How do you get into it gracefully?"

"Easier said than done," he chuckled, "but actually fairly easy when you have help..." He pushed at the floor with his foot, swung towards her, and scooped her easily off her feet to lie with her back against his chest.

Olivia flailed for a second before realizing she was actually making it more likely they'd both fall out, and relaxed back against Cory. "You could have warned me," she grumped.

"I could, but it wouldn't have been nearly as much fun." He nuzzled at her ear, making her shiver.

"Practical joker," she accused, but she couldn't repress the laughter in her voice and he knew it.

"It's a bad habit." He fell silent, and she did too, feeling oddly relaxed despite their intimately close position, despite having known him for barely twelve hours. Lying in the cradle of his thighs, head pillowed on his broad chest, Olivia felt more comfortable, more secure, than she had in a very long time. Than she could *ever* remember feeling, if she were completely honest with herself.

Cory's toe brushing the floor pushed off, set them swinging gently. The slow side-to-side motion soothed Olivia, and her eyes drifted closed.

"Are you asleep?" Cory asked quietly a few blissful minutes later.

"No." But she didn't bother to open her eyes.

"That's good." He hesitated before saying softly, "Because I'm actually a lot less sleepy than I was before you lay down on me."

She realized that the firm muscle pressed against her left ass cheek wasn't actually his thigh. It couldn't be, not unless he had three legs.

"Oh." Her eyes popped wide and her cheeks flushed with color.

"You can get up, if you like." There was a definite *or* in Cory's tone, though he didn't say the word aloud.

"I think I'm perfectly fine here, thanks."

"Mm-hm." He moved slowly, though, his hand gliding gently across her stomach and up toward her breasts, making it obvious that she could grab it and push it off at any time. Far from doing so, Olivia closed her eyes and relaxed with a soft sigh as his hand cupped her breast through her top.

Cory's warm lips nibbled at her ear as his thumb rubbed small circles over her nipple, raising it quickly to a hard little point. It was Olivia who pulled up the hem of her top, though, taking his free hand in hers and bringing it under the thin fabric to cover her other breast.

Cory made a low, hungry sound deep in his chest, fingers tightening on her nipple. "So damn tempting," he rasped against Olivia's ear, hips grinding against hers, the hardness of his arousal pressing against her ass. "Come inside with me, Olivia..."

"I think I'd probably better not," she gasped reluctantly, arching up into his tugging fingers. "It's very soon..."

He growled wordlessly. "Okay, but I want you to know I'm gonna go jack off while thinking about you."

She smiled at that, turning her head to press kisses against his stubbled jaw. "Sounds hot. I'd like to watch you do that sometime."

"Mm. I'd like to watch you pleasure yourself too." He released her breasts and moved one hand slowly across her stomach and over her shorts before curving over her mound. "How do you like to do it... fingers, or toys?"

"Battery-operated boyfriend," Olivia moaned as his fingers crooked, pressing the thin fabric against her sensitive flesh. "I... I was nervous coming through Customs with it in my suitcase, actually. I had visions of the official pulling it out and waving it around in the middle of the terminal."

Cory laughed, the rumble in his chest shaking her whole body. "I'd have liked to have seen your face."

"That's because you have a low sense of humor and find amusement in watching me make a fool of myself," Olivia tried to say the words in a sniffy, offended tone, but Cory's long fingers had just insinuated themselves inside the crotch of her boyleg shorts, grazing gently over her folds. Her voice came out breathy and high instead.

"You look beautiful whether you're fully in control or taking an unexpected header into the water," Cory murmured hotly against her ear. "But I bet you're absolutely stunning when you come." One fingertip pressed firmly against her clit, rubbing a rapid circle. Olivia bit her lip to keep from screaming with ecstasy, acutely aware that they were outside. Yes, it was dark, but anyone walking on the path past the cabins would be able to see them if she made enough noise to attract attention.

"This okay?" Cory whispered, stroking faster. She nodded jerkily against his chest, as heat spiraled through her core, every nerve starting to tingle. His other hand had never left her breast as his fingertips carried on their teasing play with her nipple. He pinched lightly as his other hand slipped lower, fingers crooking up inside her as the heel of his hand rubbed firmly over her bud.

"Oh God, Cory, yes," Olivia gasped, her grasping his wrist with both hands and holding on to it so that she could grind herself against his hand to get just the pressure she needed. "Fuck, yes, there!"

"That's it, angel," he crooned in her ear. The hammock swayed and creaked below them as Olivia shuddered with completion, biting her tongue to keep from letting out loud cries of fulfillment.

Cory hummed with contentment, leaving his fingers right where they were until Olivia finally relaxed against him, her grip on his wrist falling lax. Gently he withdrew his hand and wrapped his arms around her to hold her close in a firm embrace.

"Thank you," Olivia murmured finally.

"Think you're relaxed enough to sleep now?" he asked with a soft chuckle.

Olivia laughed. "Mm. Yes, I rather think I am. How about you?" Deliberately she wiggled her ass, pushing it against the solid bar of his erection and grinning to herself at his heartfelt groan.

"I'm not relaxed at all, but I'll be fine. I can go cool off in the shower and take care of the problem."

"I could take care of it for you," she offered. His cock twitched against her ass, straining harder against her.

"Sounds good," Cory admitted, "but this isn't exactly the best position, or location, for that."

"True. Let's go inside, then."

"Thought you weren't ready for that?"

Olivia hesitated only a second before saying, "Not quite ready to hit a home run, no, but I'd like to get you off. Only fair."

"Oh, never let it be said I denied you the chance to even the score," Cory chuckled quietly before shifting under her, bracing them with his foot on the floor, and lifting quickly. Olivia found herself on her feet almost before she knew it, Cory standing up alongside her, taking her hand in his and leading her inside.

His room was a mirror image of hers, but a lot homelier, with just a small lamp beside the bed casting everything in a softly welcoming glow. Olivia smiled on spotting the vintage *Point Break* poster framed above the bed. Of course Cory would love that movie.

"No, here." She tugged back on his hand as he led her towards the bed. She pointed at the desk instead. "Take off your shorts and sit there." She grabbed the office chair and sat down, watching as he dropped his shorts quite unselfconsciously and stood nude and magnificently male before her before backing up to the desk and seating himself on the edge of it, knees spread apart.

Olivia stared her fill for a good minute before sighing. "Damn, you're gorgeous." He truly was, all golden skin over chiseled muscle, a scattering of dark blond hair on his broad chest narrowing down to the thin happy trail bisecting those perfect abs. His cock rose, thickly engorged from a nest of dark golden curls, swollen and flushed, a pearly drop of precum just beading at the tip.

Cory smiled at her. "That's my line."

"Hush and let me admire." Olivia scooted the chair closer, laying her hands on his strong thighs and pressing them a little farther apart so she could sit in between them. Leaning in, she breathed warm air over his cock and smiled as it twitched in response.

"Christ, Olivia." Cory's hands tightened where they curled around the edge of the desk, his knuckles whitening.

She smiled up at him, holding his gaze as her lips parted, tongue slipping out to moisten them before she licked a long, slow line up the length of his cock, swiping off the bead of precum and humming with pleasure at the salty-sweet taste on her tongue.

Cory's groan was heartfelt. Olivia laughed softly before licking her lips again and opening them wide, taking the flushed, swollen head of his cock into her mouth.

"Fuck, Olivia, I'm not gonna last."

Her mouth was too full to reply, but she let her actions speak for her, taking her hands off his thighs and wrapping one of them firmly around the base of his cock, the other rolling and caressing his balls between her fingers.

Cory cried out wordlessly, his cock jerking in her fingers an instant before the first spurt hit the back of her throat. Olivia took her time, slowly sucking up every last drop before licking him clean. His hand came up to slowly caress her hair, stroking through her thick curls.

"So good," Cory said quietly, looking down at Olivia as she finally moved back and smiled up at him. "Thank you."

She smiled slow and satisfied, like a cat licking cream from its whiskers. "You're welcome. I think maybe we'll both get a good night's sleep now, hmm?" Standing, she pressed a kiss on his lips before slipping away into the night.

CHAPTER SIX

The previous day seemed dreamlike and unreal to Olivia when she woke to a bright, hot morning and Rosie knocking on her door. The other girl waited while she dressed, then accompanied her to breakfast, chattering about all the things Olivia should do on her first day.

"I'm going snorkeling later," Olivia cut Rosie off, "but I'd really like to just take a walk around the resort this morning. Find my way around properly, really get familiar with the place."

"Absolutely." Rosie nodded her approval. "Reception has a good map of the island; stop there and grab one before you go. And don't forget a hat, and sunscreen!"

Olivia thanked Rosie for her advice, refraining from snapping that she already knew that. She hadn't seen Cory this morning, at his cabin or in the staff dining room, and butterflies were beginning to flutter in her stomach. What did she really know about Cory, anyway? She'd met him less than a day ago, yet the previous night they'd got extremely hot and heavy together.

Determined to forget about Cory for the time being and get to work, she grabbed one of the maps from Reception and headed back to her cabin to put on sunscreen and find her hat and sunglasses. Ten minutes later she set off, a bag slung over her shoulder containing a bottle of water, a notebook, and a pen. In the absence of being able to take photos and make notes on her phone as she normally did, the notebook would have to do.

She kept a close eye on the time during her walk, mindful that she needed to get back to her cabin in time to change and then meet the boat at the dock at one. Lunch wasn't in her plan, since she had no desire to humiliate herself yet again in front of Cory by getting seasick on the boat. The transfer from Hamilton Island had been short enough yesterday that she hadn't worried about it, but bobbing about on a smaller boat for a couple of hours could well be a different story.

Returning to her cabin with a stack of notes to consider, she swiped another of Suzannah's sodas, thinking guiltily that she must find out where to buy more, before finding her bikini. She'd brought three, sure there would be plenty of opportunity for swimming, but no swimming shirt. Chewing on her lip, she shrugged and grabbed one of Rosie's T-shirts, an elderly-looking one. Floating facedown in the water for an hour or two, she was likely to end up with a burned back if she didn't cover up. She made sure to thickly cover every exposed inch of skin with the waterproof, high-factor sunscreen she'd bought in Sydney before putting her hat and flip-flops back on and heading for the dock.

The boat was bigger than she'd expected; not one of the big handsome cruisers that transferred tourists to and from the island, but a generously sized motor-yacht. Cory stood on the deck, talking to a couple of tourists who'd just boarded. Both were attractive young women, who stood close and gazed at him with undisguised admiration.

Cory's eyes slid towards Olivia and he smiled but made no effort to break off his conversation. She nodded at him in greeting and boarded the boat, walking past him and finding a seat on which to put her bag containing her towel and water bottle. She absolutely refused to show jealousy; quite apart from the fact that it would put Cory off her completely, she was pretty sure she didn't have anything to worry about.

Her decision was vindicated a couple of minutes later as Cory came over to greet her properly, an arm sliding around her waist as he bent to kiss her cheek and nuzzle lightly against her neck.

"Hello, beautiful."

"Hello yourself." Olivia wiggled as his fingers slid against her ribs and he found a ticklish spot. Laughing as she squeaked and danced away, Cory pulled her back closer and ducked beneath the brim of her hat to claim a proper kiss.

His lips were warm and sweet; Olivia lost herself in the kiss briefly, in the slide of the heat of his body through the thin layers of their clothing as he pulled her close.

A wolf-whistle made them pull apart. Color tinged Cory's cheeks as he made a face at the boat's driver. "Put a sock in it, Jodie."

The driver was an older woman with darkly tanned skin and white teeth flashing in her laughing face. Cory introduced Olivia, telling her, "Jodie's spent her whole life in the Whitsunday Islands. She knows all the best snorkel and dive spots, and nobody's better at finding the whales in whale-watching season."

"Which is when?" Olivia asked curiously.

"June to August is the best time. The whales give birth to their calves in the warm waters here;

it's a natural nursery for them. We're not allowed to get too close, but sometimes they come close to us." Jodie smiled at her. "I've got some amazing photos and video we've taken off the boat; you can have whatever you like for marketing material."

"That's terrific!" Olivia said. Cory had remained at her side, his warm hand resting lightly on the small of her back. He moved away then with a murmured apology to go and greet some more tourists boarding the boat. Olivia barely noticed his departure, focused on her conversation with Jodie.

"That everyone, Cory?" Jodie called back after a couple of minutes. "Cast off, then!" she said when she got a reply in the affirmative.

"Do you need me to sit down?" Olivia asked uncertainly.

"No, you're fine there." Jodie expertly brought the boat's big engines up to a low rev, guiding the boat away from the dock with a deft touch. "You two look good together," she said unexpectedly.

"We only met yesterday," Olivia admitted, "but I feel like I'm falling head over heels."

"I've known that boy all his life." Jodie was wearing reflective sunglasses, so Olivia couldn't see her eyes, but her tone was friendly. "He's one of the few people I've ever met who's just as beautiful on the inside as the outside. Don't you break his heart, now."

"I'll try," Olivia promised, touched by Jodie's obvious fondness for Cory. Nobody seemed to have a bad word to say about him, except Jill who obviously had an ax to grind. "It'd be like kicking a puppy—how could you? I've got baggage, though. Maybe too much."

"Eh." Jodie shrugged, gunning the engines as they cleared the small harbor. "That's life for you. You'll do fine. You didn't look funny at him when those girls were all over him; that's the one thing Cory wouldn't be able to stand."

"Rosie warned me about that," Olivia admitted. They were having to speak more loudly to be heard over the engine noise, and she looked towards the back of the boat, hoping Cory wouldn't overhear. He was talking cheerfully to a young couple, though, helping them select snorkeling gear from a cabinet. "She told me about Jill."

"Did she now!" Jodie said nothing more, though, just concentrated on piloting the boat, and Olivia relaxed and turned her attention to the crystal blue waters they skimmed rapidly across.

"Hey." Cory came to join her a few minutes later, slipping into the empty seat beside her and putting his arm around her shoulders. "Want to come pick out some snorkeling gear? Everyone else has theirs."

"Sure." She followed him to the back of the boat, ignoring the two girls who'd been flirting with Cory and who were now staring at her and whispering to each other. *They are no threat to me*, she told herself and believed it. Even knowing Cory as little as she did, she was quite certain the chance of him getting involved with one of the resorts guests was pretty much zero.

"How long does the boat trip take?" she called to Cory over the engine noise, which was even louder at the back of the boat.

"About twenty minutes," he called back, picking up a set of flippers and holding them close to her feet, nodding that he thought they were about the right size. She chose a mask and snorkel.

"This'll do."

"Got sunscreen on?"

"All over. I don't need a burn on my first full day."

"Damn."

She looked a query at him; he laughed, hooked an arm around her waist, and pulled her close. "I was hoping to be able to offer to help you apply it."

"Lecher," Olivia accused, laughing back up at him.

"You're mad if you think I'd pass up a chance to put my hands all over this gorgeous body of yours." He bent his head to bring his lips to hers, but Olivia let him claim only a brief kiss before pulling back.

"You're working, Cory. And so am I. I want to talk to some of the guests about what they like best about Sunfish Island. Get some idea of what draws people here in the first place." She gave him an apologetic smile, and he let her go with no sign of reluctance.

"Damn, I love smart women who are right all the time."

She gave him a pert smile for that remark before whirling away, snorkeling gear in hand, to go and get started on her job. It would be easy to get carried away in her romance with Cory, but that wasn't why she was here. She was being given a chance to repair her ruined professional reputation, a chance she'd never get anywhere else, and she had no intention of throwing that away.

Olivia was sitting and chatting with a friendly middle-aged couple when the engines slowed to a gentle throb. Looking out the window beside her, she saw they had drawn up to a small pontoon, which was obviously moored in place. Cory was standing on it and tied off a rope before he gave Jodie a thumbs-up and the engines died altogether.

The sudden silence was almost overwhelming. Cory and Jodie leaped into action, urging everyone off the boat and onto the pontoon, where Cory gave a quick talk about safety, warning everyone not to touch the coral and to stay within sight of the pontoon.

"We're in a bay with very little current, but if you get into any difficulty, turn over onto your back and raise your hand in the air, and I'll come get you," he concluded.

"Aren't you coming in, Cory?" one of his admirers asked.

"Afraid not. Jodie and I are your lifeguards. We're responsible for every one of you, so we'll be staying right here, watching over you. Now has everyone got their sunscreen on? Don't want any red lobsters coming back out of this water!"

There was a general chorus of agreement, then Cory gave them the go-ahead to enter the water. Olivia went in eagerly, keen to see the world-famous reef, although of course she was only seeing a tiny, tiny corner of the World Heritage Site here.

Almost instantly she found herself swimming through a school of tiny, brightly colored fish darting in and out of the coral. A manta ray lifted up from a patch of sand not far away and flew majestically through the turquoise water, wings sweeping slowly up and down.

She saw a new wonder everywhere she looked. She was a strong swimmer, so she had no problem staying under for a good amount of time, blowing bubbles and swimming with long, smooth kicks of her fins to propel herself through the water. It would be easy to lose track of time down here, she thought with a start when she surfaced to get a few deep breaths, checked the time, and found that almost an hour had passed already. She'd swum quite some distance from the pontoon; looking back at it, she found Cory peering towards her. He gave her a wave and she waved back before popping her mouthpiece back in and going facedown in the water again, heading back towards the pontoon this time.

"Enjoying yourself?" Cory said with a grin down at her as she surfaced near his feet.

"This is incredible," Olivia gave him a glowing, happy smile, pulling her mask off. "I mean, I've seen pictures, but I always assumed they were the exception—selected highlights, you know. Not the norm. But it's just as perfect down there as in every picture I've ever seen."

"You really have to go diving with Bryce. The outer reefs have even more variety." Cory reached for a large cooler he'd brought from the boat. "Want to hop out and have a drink of water? We've got about another half hour."

She accepted his offer of a hand out and sat on the edge of the pontoon, dangling her feet in the water as she drained the bottle of water he gave her.

"Hand me the bottle," Cory requested as she finished. "Gotta make sure we take all our rubbish back with us."

"Of course."

"Going back in?" He'd stayed standing beside her, but he wasn't looking at her, his eyes constantly scanning over the water checking on the other snorkelers instead. He took his job seriously, which Olivia genuinely appreciated. She wouldn't have wanted a man who flirted while he was supposed to be looking out for the safety of others.

She went back into the water for another swim and mainly floated along the surface this time, watching the schools of brightly colored fish darting among the coral and thinking that when she went into town to buy a new laptop, she'd have to have a look at waterproof cameras. An Instagram was just one of the ideas she planned to implement for Sunfish, and posting new photos from the Reef every day would be a big draw.

CHAPTER SEVEN

On the way back to the resort, everyone was quiet, tired from their exertions. Olivia sat staring vaguely out over the blue water, her mind whirling with plans. She barely noticed when Cory sat down alongside her, but when he casually put his arm around her shoulders, she flinched with sudden pain.

"Ouch!"

Startled, he pulled back. "Olivia? Are you okay?"

His arm had really hurt when it pressed against her, and now that she was thinking on it, the skin all over her shoulders and back felt sore and tight.

"Oh my God. I'm such an idiot."

He leaned back and looked at her, at the T-shirt she was wearing over her bikini. The white T-shirt, which was drying out now and was no longer quite as alluringly transparent as it had been earlier.

"You forgot to put sunscreen on under the T-shirt, didn't you? Forgot that you'd burn through it once it got wet."

"I'm such an idiot," she said again, tears starting in her eyes.

"Shush, it's okay. It happens. Look, when we get back, go straight to your cabin and take a cool shower, okay? I'll help Jodie clear the boat and I'll come straight over with a bottle of aloe. We'll get you through it." He pressed a light kiss to her brow.

"Olivia?" Cory tapped gently on her screen door. The glass door to the inside of the cabin was open, but the drapes were drawn behind it. "Can I come in?"

"Yeah," came the soft reply, and he opened the screen to enter, pushing aside the drapes.

She lay facedown on the bed, wearing only a pair of cotton bikini panties. Cory sucked in a breath at the state of her back, broken by the white lines where her bikini had covered her. The sunscreen had done its job on the backs of her thighs, and she'd obviously worked it up onto her shoulders as well, but her lower and upper back were an angry red.

"Oh, honey. You're gonna be really sore for a few days."

"Don't rub it in." She turned her head to the side, resting her cheek on the pillow, and stared at him. "Or rather, if that's aloe you've got in that bottle, do rub it in. Lots of it."

"Certainly is." She was in the middle of the bed, so Cory had plenty of room to sit down on the edge, crack open the bottle, and pour a generous amount of aloe into the middle of her back. "This isn't exactly the way I'd hoped to get my hands all over your beautiful body," he teased as he gently smoothed the thick gel over her burned skin.

"Wasn't what I had in mind either," Olivia griped, "but since it feels really good, I'm not complaining." She smiled crookedly up at him, and he couldn't resist leaning down to kiss her. "You'll need to do it at least a couple of times a day until I'm all better too," she added cheekily when he straightened back up, and Cory couldn't help but laugh. God, she was a delight; he'd been attracted to her from the moment he saw her, but in getting to know her, he realized she was so much more than just an admittedly very pretty face.

"I am your willing slave," he jested, pouring on some more aloe when he saw that her skin had already soaked in the first application. "You should really stay here under the air conditioner for tonight at least; can I get you something to eat? More water?" He saw an almost empty water bottle on the night stand; at least she was drinking. She'd need to.

"Both, please. I skipped lunch because I was worried about getting seasick and I'm starving," Olivia confessed.

"No headache?" A headache could indicate sunstroke as well as the burn, but she shook her head.

"Honestly, I feel fine apart from an extremely sore back."

He finished smoothing the thick gel into her back, then went into her bathroom to wash his hands. "I'll be back in a bit with some food. Anything in particular?" He recalled that she had a good appetite, having seen her eat lunch yesterday. He wouldn't skimp on the portion.

"Anything, I'm not fussy." Olivia shrugged and winced as the movement tugged at her sore skin. "Could you get me some more water? There's a jug in the fridge in there." She waved a hand vaguely at the door that led into the lounge.

"Gotcha." Cory picked up the near-empty bottle, headed into the next room, and came face-to-face with Suzannah. She raised her eyebrows, looking past him at Olivia lying facedown on her bed in only a pair of panties.

"Well, you certainly move fast, surfer boy," she drawled, looking amused and highly entertained.

"It's not like that. She's got a sunburn."

Suzannah's smirk vanished at once. "*Merde*, on her first day? How did you manage that, Olivia?" She pushed past Cory and bent over Olivia with a concerned frown. "Oh, that is going to hurt."

"Already does, but Cory's been generous with the aloe." Olivia gave her roommate a wry smile. "My fault. I forgot I'd burn through my T-shirt once it got wet, and didn't put sunscreen on my back before I went snorkeling."

Cory came back in with the water bottle and set it down on the nightstand. "I'm gonna go get her some dinner," he said. "Are you working tonight, Suze?" He suspected he knew the answer; the restaurants were just about to open and the chef would have already been in action for quite a while if she were on duty.

"No." Suze shook her head. "My night off. Which is good, I can keep Olivia company and we can get to know each other, yes? In fact, if you are going to be room service waiter, Cory, you could bring me some as well." She grinned at him, and he threw his hands up in surrender, laughing.

"I shall return!"

"You comfortable?" Suzannah asked as soon as Cory was gone. "Need more aloe?"

"Has it soaked in already?" Olivia groaned when Suzannah confirmed it had. "Yes, please. But just to clarify, I had no problem with Cory being here and rubbing it in for me."

Suzannah laughed throatily as she picked up the aloe bottle Cory had left behind. "Trust me, sugar, I wouldn't have a problem with that hunk of delicious man rubbing his hands all over my naked body either!"

Olivia couldn't help but giggle at Suzannah's remark, delivered in her thick French accent that could have made reciting the telephone directory sound unbearably sensual. Suzannah had brought in her laptop, and the two girls lay side by side on the bed, swapping favorite websites, when Cory returned bearing a covered tray.

"It's amazing what results I get when casually mentioning that this was for you, Suzannah," he said, hooking an ankle around a chair and pulling it up to the end of the bed. "Why do I have the feeling all your kitchen staff are terrified of you?"

"Because they are," she replied, perfectly unruffled. "If a chef's staff are not calling her a tyrant when her back is turned, she is not doing her job properly."

Olivia and Cory just looked at each other.

"You'll never understand, so don't try," Olivia warned. "I did some marketing campaigns for restaurants in New York. The chefs are a law unto themselves, and it's pretty much expected. I don't think they live in the same world as the rest of us."

"We live in the world of good food," Suzannah said regally, claiming the bags Cory had brought with him and opening them, sniffing inside each and wrinkling her nose. "Let us see what offerings my followers believe are fit for consumption tonight."

Cory tactfully headed into the lounge while Olivia sat up and pulled on a loose shirt. He returned with plates and cutlery, dragging the table over to the end of the bed so Suzannah could lay the food out on it. She sent him back to collect soda from the fridge, and he grinned at her.

"I can do better than that. I've got beer at my place."

"Fetch." Suzannah flipped her hand at him.

Olivia giggled as Cory trotted off to do Suzannah's bidding. "You are so bossy. Does everyone just ask how high when you say jump?"

"Why would they not?" Suzannah arched her brows curiously.

"Wow, I admire your confidence. Do you have a boyfriend?"

"*Non*. I intimidate a lot of men." Suzannah gave a very Gallic shrug. "But if a man is intimidated by me, then he is not man enough for me anyway. I'd prefer no man at all than a weak one." She slid a plate over to Olivia. "Here. Tell me what you think of these."

Cory returned with a six-pack of cold beers, setting one down in front of each of the two girls and twisting the tops off. "Would you like a glass?" he checked with Olivia, suddenly wondering if she would think they were uncultured for drinking directly from the bottle.

"No, it's fine." She smiled up at him, picked up the bottle, and took a long sip.

Olivia couldn't remember the last time she'd such an enjoyable evening. The food Suzannah's staff had sent her was absolutely amazing, the beer ice-cold, and the company excellent. They must have been making enough noise to sound like quite a party, because Rosie soon tapped on the screen door and came in to join them. Bryce, the dive instructor, followed not long after, though Cory promptly sent him back out for more beers.

"I think she's asleep."

Olivia roused enough to mutter, "No 'm not," and heard Cory's quiet laugh.

"Yes, you are, angel. Shh. I've kicked everyone out. Let's get that shirt off and I'll put some more aloe on your back before you sleep."

"I can do that," Suzannah's accented voice said, but Olivia waved her off, sitting up to fumble at her shirt buttons.

"No offense, but I like Cory's hands on me better."

Suzannah laughed, nudging Cory. "All right, but you, keep those hands on the burned parts only, hmm?"

"Scout's honor," he promised.

"Do you even have Boy Scouts here in Australia?" She was maybe a little bit drunk, Olivia realized, as her words slightly slurred. She'd only had three beers but that was a lot more than she usually drank these days. In her time at the center of the social whirl of New York, she'd probably had a much higher alcohol tolerance.

"Yes, we do. Need the bathroom? Come on, those teeth want scrubbing." Cory helped her up and into the bathroom, going back out to give her privacy but not quite closing the door, insisting she keep talking to him. When she came back out and gave him a grumpy look, he even managed to keep his eyes on her face and not her exposed breasts as he led her back to bed and helped her get comfortable on her stomach.

"You're such a sweet guy," Olivia mumbled as he poured more aloe on her back and smoothed it in gently.

"I'll be honest and say that my thoughts are not at all sweet at the moment." He lightly stroked the two dimples on either side of the base of her spine. "And that if you weren't so badly burned, me giving you a back massage would be a prelude to something other than sleep."

Olivia smiled into her pillow. "Can I get a rain check on that?"

"Anytime." She felt a gentle kiss on her nape, then Cory drew the sheet gently up over her. "Get some sleep, Olivia. And stay out of the sun tomorrow!"

"Stay," she said impulsively as his weight lifted off the bed.

"Hmm?"

"Would you stay? And just sleep here?"

"You sure?"

"Yes, please."

"Give me five minutes." He left her alone but was back in less than the time he'd promised, breath smelling freshly of toothpaste. Wearing a

T-shirt and boxers, he slid into bed beside her. "This okay?"

Cheek turned towards him on the pillow, Olivia gave him a sleepy smile. "Perfect."

"Sleep well then, angel." He leaned over to kiss her lips gently before turning out the light.

CHAPTER EIGHT

Olivia woke with a sore, a stinging back, and an exceptionally comfortable front. At some point during the night, she'd apparently migrated completely atop Cory and now lay with her cheek on his chest, head tucked under his chin, breasts pressed against his rock-hard abs, their legs tangled together. It could scarcely be a more intimate position.

Cory was still asleep, his broad chest rising and falling slowly. It was a comforting rhythm, and if Olivia hadn't been so sore, she'd probably have been soothed straight back to sleep. As it was, one of his broad hands was splayed across the small of her back and she felt hot and sweaty. Edging carefully off him, she headed for the bathroom.

"What time is it?" Cory mumbled sleepily as she returned.

"Almost six," she replied quietly, checking her watch.

"Ugh, I gotta get up. I'm taking a group on a rainforest hike." He sat up, eying her appreciatively in the early morning light filtering past the blinds. Olivia smirked at him as she sat on the bed, making no effort to cover her bare breasts.

"Getting a good view there?"

"Magnificent," he breathed, eyes riveted as she deliberately took a few deep breaths. Giving himself a shake, he reached to the nightstand. "But I know the back view won't be pretty. Down on your face, angel."

She lay down without a word, extremely keen to get another soothing layer of aloe on her back. The skin felt hot and tight; she hadn't gotten much of a glimpse in the dimly lit bathroom when she peered over her shoulder at herself in the mirror, but enough to know that her back was practically glowing.

"You should really stay here and rest today," Cory said, generously slathering the aloe over her back. "I'll get someone to bring you some breakfast and check in on you through the day. I've got a really busy one scheduled, unfortunately. I'll get some more aloe for you too."

"I don't want to be a bother, and really, I should get up..."

"You should absolutely not. I saw Luke last night when I was fetching dinner and told him you'd got a nasty burn; if he sees you around the resort today, he'll be ordering your ass back to bed, so you may as well stay here."

"I'll go mad with boredom!" Olivia protested mutinously.

"No, you won't, because Suze left you her laptop." Cory gestured to where it sat on the desk. "She'll have it connected to the resort's staff Wi-Fi too, so you can binge on Netflix all you like."

"Netflix and chill?" Olivia gave him a wicked grin as he moved away, heading for the bathroom to wash his hands.

"In the most literal use of the term, yeah." He grinned over his shoulder at her, so she knew he was aware of the colloquial meaning. "But when you're better, I would love to Netflix and chill with you."

Cory dropped a kiss on her cheek and smoothed her hair before departing. "Try and get some more sleep," he said before closing the screen door quietly behind him.

Feeling wide awake, Olivia thought she wouldn't go back to sleep, but she must have dozed off, because the next thing she knew, there was a quiet tapping on the screen door.

"Olivia, you awake?"

"Uh-huh," she managed vaguely. It was a woman's voice, so she didn't worry about pulling a sheet over her, though she wished she had when the door slid open and Jill came in.

"Hey." Jill set a tray down on the desk. "How are you doing... oh wow, that is some burn. Cory wasn't exaggerating."

Her back felt sore again; too much so to hold on to her pride. "Would you put some more aloe on for me?" Olivia begged pathetically.

"Of course. Cory told me to bring more." Jill held up a fresh bottle. Her expression looked genuinely sympathetic, Olivia thought. "I'm sorry."

Did her words have more than one meaning? She sounded contrite rather than just sympathetic. "What for?" Olivia asked as Jill squirted a fresh glob of aloe onto her back.

"I've been a bitch, and you didn't deserve it."

Olivia lay silent for a moment before saying, "I feel like someone's read you the riot act. Was it Cory?"

"Rosie, actually. She said you were really nice and it's none of my business who Cory wants to date. Which is absolutely true." Jill's hands stilled on her back. "He's not really a player, if you hadn't figured it out yet."

"I was pretty sure."

"Yeah, it's pretty obvious." Jill sighed and got up, going to wash her hands. "I'm not really still in love with him," she said, returning and sitting at the desk, reaching to put the tray beside Olivia on the bed. "I was just... jealous that he's finally moving on. He hadn't so much as looked at anyone in ages."

Olivia said nothing, just picked up the sealed cup of orange juice on the tray and opened it. The tray held a covered plate that contained a still-warm croissant and a flaky Danish, a little pat of butter on one side. "I don't suppose your olive branch extends to making me a coffee, does it?" she asked hopefully.

Jill's worried expression eased and she laughed. "Of course it does," she said warmly. "I think I owe you a few, to be frank. How do you like it?"

"Well, my regular barista back on the corner of Madison Avenue and East 32nd Street used to make me an amazing cinnamon-vanilla macchiato," Olivia said and couldn't hold in her laughter at Jill's horrified expression. "Milk and no sugar will be perfect."

Jill giggled too as she went to put the kettle on. "For a moment there I thought I was getting belted in the face with that olive branch!"

Olivia quickly discovered that she liked Jill a lot. The other girl was sharply witty and great fun to be around when her jealousy wasn't eating her alive. Jill shyly asked if Olivia would like some company as she didn't have anywhere to be that morning. Later she mentioned she was working late that day, as she was taking the boat into Airlie Beach to collect a large group that was arriving at the mainland airport in the early evening.

"I want to go." Olivia desperately needed to go clothes shopping, and to replace the electronics that had been drowned in her fall off the boat.

"Cory said you should stay here..."

"Are you serious? Cory is definitely not the boss of me. I'll be fine. I'll cover every inch of skin, I promise... and I'll stick to you like glue so I don't get lost."

Jill snickered. "I suppose I could show you the good shops. Some of them are a bit too touristy and expensive. The boat goes in earlier to deliver the departing tourists to the airport, so we could have a good couple hours before we need to collect the new arrivals."

"Sounds like a plan. What time do we have to leave?"

Jill still took a bit of persuading, but Olivia eventually convinced her that she would go mad if she had to stay in bed all day. She found a button-down denim shirt in the things Rosie had loaned her and put it on without a bra—the straps would have been too painful on her sore skin. Fortunately she wasn't so well-endowed that she'd bounce. A pair of long linen trousers from her own wardrobe, a large sunhat and sunglasses, and Jill pronounced her safe to go outside.

Several hours later, tired but content, Olivia was half drowsing when Jill nudged her.

"Think you might have a small problem."

"Hm?" She jolted out of her doze, looked where Jill was pointing as the boat came in to dock. "Oh dear." Cory's height and blond hair were unmistakable, as was the way he paced up and down the dock. "Do you think he's gonna be a grump because I didn't obey his orders to stay in bed?"

"Not once he sees that you're perfectly fine, no." Jill grinned at her. "I highly recommend grabbing him and sticking your tongue down his throat to cut off any tirade before he gets started, though."

"Good idea, because I'll probably smack his face if he tries to boss me around!" The two girls were fast friends after spending the afternoon together. Jill had kept her word to show Olivia the shops, and helped to carry the bags full of her purchases back to the boat before they headed for the airport, and in turn Olivia had helped Jill corral the arriving guests and get them all organized.

Cory seemed to be struggling with himself as he watched Olivia disembark laden with shopping bags. She walked towards him a little hesitantly, offered up a small smile.

"Shopping? Really?" he said resignedly.

"You did witness all my electronics getting drowned." She waved the bag containing her new laptop, tablet, and mobile phone at him. "Plus, I really need some Sunfish-appropriate clothing. Can't be wearing Rosie's stuff all the time."

He sighed, and to his credit said not one word about her promise to stay in her room. Which technically, she hadn't actually given, Olivia thought virtuously. Instead, he just held out his hands. "Can I carry those for you?"

Olivia beamed at him and unloaded the heavier bags from her haul. "You earn lots of brownie points for that, you realize."

"I was hoping. Is there a reward?" Cory smiled at last.

"There could be." She gave him a coquettish look. "But it'll have to be delivered in private."

Cory walked very quickly, long legs eating up the ground as he headed purposefully back to the staff accommodation area. Laughing her ass off, Olivia followed. By the time she caught up, he was unpacking her electronics purchases on her desk.

"Figured I'd save you some time. Now, about that reward?"

"Well"—she deposited her own bags on the chair—"you get to put your hands all over me again."

"How's that back?" He came over to gently ease her shirt off her shoulders as she unfastened the buttons, hissing softly between his teeth as he saw her back. "Still red as hell, but it *does* look a bit better, I think."

"I want a shower. Want to come in and wash my back?" She cast him a coquettish look over her shoulder. Catching her waist in his hands, Cory pressed a kiss to her shoulder before seeking her lips.

"Definitely," he said, voice dropping to a low husk. "I'll wash any body part you like. All of them."

"Sounds good to me." Dropping her shorts and panties, she darted ahead of him into the bathroom. Cory didn't hesitate in giving chase, though he drew the line at hopping under the shower as she stepped straight under it, hissing with pleasure as the cool water rained down on her back.

"You are one hardcore ballsy babe," he said admiringly, stopping to shuck his own clothes.

Olivia peered at him from underneath the spray. "What does that even mean?"

"It means I'm crazy about you, you beautiful, crazy, impulsive woman." His eyes moved to her breasts, where her nipples had peaked hard in the cold water. It was starting to warm up, though, so he stepped in with her and closed the shower screen, sliding his arms around her and bending his head to kiss her as she tilted her face up to smile at him.

Olivia moved into Cory's arms confidently as the water warmed. She'd set the mixer tap only to lukewarm, but it was a hot day and any warmer than that would feel unpleasant on her burned back anyway. His lips were soft on hers at first, then more demanding as she parted them and flicked her tongue against his. Her hands landed on his arms and gripped the thick muscles of his biceps, fingertips exploring the way his skin felt beneath her touch.

His hands avoided the tender skin of her back by going straight down to grasp her ass and pull her flush against his body. His cock was hard, pressing against her belly, and the hair on his chest rubbed against her breasts, stimulating her nipples. She closed her eyes, melting against him; her whole body felt sensitive, every touch magnified. Heat gathered between her thighs, but there was no rush, no hurry. She reached for her shower gel and squirted some into her hand, reaching up to rub it into Cory's chest.

"Let's get you all clean," Olivia said, her voice coming out low and husky.

"Before we get really, really dirty?" Cory said hopefully, taking the bottle from her.

"Works for me." She turned as he tugged on her hip, letting him soap her back gently and remove the residue of sticky aloe there. He nuzzled his cheek against her hair and nibbled lightly on the tip of her ear. Olivia's mouth opened in a soft gasp as she leaned back against him.

Cory's hands moved slow but sure as they glided from her hips over her stomach, slick with soap suds, and curved under her breasts to cup them gently before his thumbs flicked over her nipples.

Olivia hummed with pleasure, rocking her head sideways against Cory's shoulder so she could reach up to kiss him. He had to lean down for their lips to meet, not that she minded in the slightest. They kissed slow and sensual, tongues dancing with each other as Cory caressed her breasts, squeezing and rolling her nipples between fingers and thumbs until she moaned and ground her ass back against the heavy erection he pressed against her.

He lifted his head to look down at her, his blue eyes dark with passion. "Olivia." His voice was deeper, a husky note in it.

"Yes." He hadn't asked a question, but the answer was still inevitable. There was no soap on them now, and she turned the shower off, took his hand, and led him back to the bedroom, both of them still dripping water. She paused only to grab one of her bags from her shopping haul and fish out the large box of condoms.

Cory grinned at the sight. "Good plan."

"Yup, and here's another. Lie down."

"Want to be on top, huh? I can live with that." He eased onto the bed and reclined comfortably, gazing up at her with appreciation as she tore into the plastic wrapper on the condom box. "Probably easier on your back too."

"That had entered into my thinking," she admitted, extracting a single foil packet and tossing the box onto the nightstand.

Cory's cock stood stiff and proud from a nest of dark golden curls. Olivia stroked it a few times, enjoying the way he gasped and shifted at her touch and how his blue eyes darkened before he caught her wrist and pulled her towards him. "Come here," he requested, reaching down and stroking lightly up her thigh. "Come sit on my face."

"Oh... it's okay, I..."

"I want to taste you," Cory admitted, looking up at her. "Come here, Olivia."

A flush rose to her cheeks, but she nodded, climbing onto the bed and moving to straddle his face. He curled his arms around her thighs, shifting down slightly on the pillows, humming with appreciation as he positioned himself just right.

"So pretty," he murmured before his tongue flicked out, lapping gently over her folds, forming into a point to nudge back the hood of her clit.

"Oh my God." The bed had no headboard, so Olivia had to place her hands on the wall to try to steady herself. Cory knew exactly what he was doing with his tongue, and he lost no time in driving her absolutely crazy, to the point where she ended up shoving one of her own hands in her mouth to try to muffle her shrieks of pleasure.

"You're delightfully noisy," Cory murmured, easily shifting her down his body until she straddled his hips, though he was careful to make sure his cock went between them, pressing against her stomach. Olivia could only gasp and shudder before collapsing to lie on his broad chest.

"Okay there?" Cory kept his hands away from her sore back, stroking his fingertips in slow, rhythmic circles on the outsides of her thighs instead as her breathing gradually slowed.

"No," Olivia said.

"No?" There was laughter in his voice as he kissed her hair.

"Too good," she sighed, shifting languorously against him. "That mouth of yours is absolutely wicked."

Pleased with himself, Cory was quite happy to just hold her for a while, though his cock ached to plunge deep into her. At length she stilled her small movements and lifted her head to look at him. Her smile was absolutely glorious, and he gazed at her, spellbound by her beauty. At least until she wriggled back, reaching for the condoms, and tore one of the packets open.

"Aahh, so good." Cords stood out in Cory's neck as he flung his head back, gritting his teeth. Olivia laughed softly as she rolled the condom on, stroking both hands down firmly, pausing to caress over his tightly swollen balls.

"Something you need?"

"Damn right there is!" His hands closed on her hips and he lifted her, shifting to push up against her. She kept one hand wrapped around the base of his cock until she'd guided the head right where she wanted it.

Cory groaned as Olivia sank slowly down onto him, his cock sliding deep into her tight, wet channel. She hummed with pleasure, pushing down hard to take him fully inside and rocking her hips, setting up a rhythm that was going to get him off pretty damn quickly.

"Jeez, Olivia, slow down," he gasped, sliding a hand between them to find her clit and slide a finger over it. She moaned but didn't obey his request, her curls bouncing as she rode him rapidly to a mutual climax as satisfying as either of them could possibly have wanted.

Afterwards, Olivia lay on Cory's chest, listening to the thump of his heartbeat below her ear as it steadied back to a normal rhythm. His hands lay loosely on her upper thighs; even in the throes of orgasm, he hadn't touched her sore back, and her heart swelled with affection for him, for his consideration and his gentleness.

When she'd fled New York with her tail metaphorically between her legs, she'd hoped for merely somewhere safe and quiet to lick her wounds, far from the glare of the spotlight and the tattered remains of her career. She'd never thought for a moment that she might be lucky enough to find friends like Rosie, Suzannah, and Jill; never dared to dream she might find a man like Cory, who was willing to take a chance on a relationship with her even knowing everything about her past.

Lying there listening to Cory's breathing slow as he drifted towards sleep, Olivia knew a contentment she'd never before experienced. Here on the far side of the world, on a tropical island far removed from where she'd ever expected she might end up, she'd finally found *home*.

Letting her eyes close, Olivia let herself drift off to sleep, held securely in Cory's arms. Whatever the future might hold for the two of them—and she hoped that it held a great deal—she knew that no matter what, she would always have a place with her friends on Sunfish Island.

~ The End ~

FINDING CORY

THE RELUCTANT BILLIONAIRE

Island Escapes Book 2

CHAPTER ONE

The warm wind blowing in Jace Hunter's face tasted of salt. Licking it off his lips, he closed his eyes and tilted his face up to soak in the sunlight beaming down on him. The heat felt good on his skin; he almost felt as though he was able to directly absorb the energy, like a plant. A small smile crossed his face at the whimsical thought.

"We're pulling in to the dock now," a voice announced through a speaker right above his head. Startled, his eyes snapped open and he glared at the offending machine. Not that it stopped the voice from continuing, "Welcome to Sunfish Island, folks!"

There were about a dozen other guests on the boat. Jace let them all depart first before pushing himself to his feet and shouldering his duffel bag. A deckhand was unloading suitcases onto the dock; Jace snagged his in passing and handed the young man a five dollar bill.

"Thanks, sir." The deckhand looked surprised to be given a tip. "American, are you?"

Jace shook his head. "No, but I've been living there for a while. Got in the habit of tipping. You've earned it, those cases look heavy." He nodded to the stack with his chin. "Have yourself a cold beer on me."

At the end of the dock, the guests were being greeted by resort staff, then directed to the main reception to check in and get their rooms assigned. A tall man looked in Jace's direction, started toward him, paused, and looked him up and down with a puzzled frown.

"Luke?" Jace offered a smile.

"It *is* you!" Puzzlement gave way to a wide grin. "I didn't recognize you!" Luke Collyer was Sunfish Island's general manager, an extremely competent, likable man. Jace had been involved in hiring him two years ago and the two men had taken to each other at once.

Jace shrugged wearily, shaking Luke's offered hand. "It's been a rough few weeks." That was an understatement. He'd been laid low by a nasty bout of the flu, but had tried to work through it, refusing to accept his own physical weakness. It wasn't until he'd collapsed in the middle of an important meeting, waking up in the hospital on oxygen, that he'd accepted he might not be at peak fitness.

The doctors had diagnosed pneumonia, kept him in hospital for a solid week, and finally let him go with a stern admonition to take a break. He'd fully intended to ignore them and go right back to work… except when Jace had walked in the door of his office on the top floor of Hunter Enterprises' New York skyscraper, his father had been sitting behind his desk.

John Hunter had built Hunter Enterprises from nothing to a multi-billion-dollar, diversified business empire. His devoted wife Maryann had been at his side the whole way, until her death from cancer five years earlier. Jace was their only son, the heir to everything. Living up to his father's expectations was something he'd spent his whole life doing, and John Hunter was a workaholic.

So it had come as quite a shock when John had stood up and said, "Get your ass out of this office, and don't you dare set foot in here again until you have your health back!"

Jace had laughed, but his father was deadly serious. "Your mother ignored her symptoms for too long. I won't see you sacrifice your health to this business, Jace. Get out of here. Go and smell the roses for a while."

His father had bulldozed over every argument Jace had tried to make, and truth to tell, Jace hadn't really tried all that hard. The Hunter Enterprises private jet had been on standby to take him anywhere he'd wanted to go. He hadn't been able to think of anywhere until his father had suggested the family's private villa on Sunfish Island, the resort island on Australia's Great Barrier Reef, which Hunter Enterprises had bought out and redeveloped a few years earlier. Jace had actually designed the villa as his graduation project for his architecture degree, but he'd never had the time to go and see the completed work.

"Your father said you'd been ill, but you look terrible," Luke said, jerking Jace from his reverie.

"Thanks," Jace said wryly, but he knew it was true. He'd lost a lot of weight during his illness. The tailored suits he customarily wore hung loosely on his frame; he'd left them behind in New York and brought shorts and T-shirts for his vacation. The dark blond hair he normally kept neatly trimmed had grown out long and shaggy, and he had several days' growth of beard on his face. He was unrecognizable from the high-powered businessman he'd been just a few weeks ago.

Which gave him an idea.

"Luke," he asked as they came to a parked golf cart and Luke hefted his case into the back, "who knows I'm here?"

Luke shot him a knowing look. "Only me. Your father called and asked me to have the villa opened up for you, but my staff don't know who's expected. You want me to keep it quiet?"

"I think it might be best. I don't particularly want the press getting wind that I'm here, Hunter Enterprises is privately owned so it's not like there's a stock price to crash, but still…"

"Jace, you don't need to give me a reason. It's all good." Luke handed him a plastic card. "Here."

"What's this?"

"It's a comp card. It means you don't pay for anything, anywhere, at any of the bars and restaurants. You own the place, after all." Luke's grin was cheerful. "It'd be a bit dumb to ask you to pay for anything. This way, you don't have to sign for anything; we're a cashless economy here, you'll recall?"

"Like a cruise ship." Jace nodded. "So, if I use this card, there's no need to use the villa's account, and no need to put my name on anything."

"And nobody to be alerted to your identity." Luke steered the golf cart along a paved path winding among groves of palm trees. "Housekeeping opened the villa up and stocked your kitchen, but I'll advise them that a family friend is using the place. If you want maid service, just let me know and I'll have somebody come in when you're out. Just one question, if I may?"

The sea glinted blue on their left as they ascended a slope, moving away from the main resort; Jace knew they were approaching the non-resort part of the island, where some two dozen exclusive private villas had been built. A couple of them were occupied by permanent residents, but the rest were holiday homes for the mega-rich. He wasn't likely to be afflicted with nosy neighbors.

"What's the question?" he asked, gazing at the glorious view of the sunlit Coral Sea opening up before them as they reached the top of the rise.

"How long are you staying? And do you need medical support while you're here?"

"That's two… but I'll answer. I shouldn't need any medical attention, no, and I expect to stay a couple of weeks, probably. Dad told me not to show my face at any Hunter Enterprises office again before two weeks is up."

"That doesn't include *my* office," Luke said with a grin. "Stop by anytime you want a chat, but I'll have no compunctions about telling you to butt out of resort business."

"Deal." Jace smiled back at Luke as the golf cart drew to a halt, thinking it would be nice to have a friend here he could talk to. Nice to have a friend to talk to at all, if he was being completely honest with himself. The cutthroat world of big business wasn't exactly conducive to close personal friendships.

*   *   *

Laying on the couch binge-watching Netflix was something he could only do for so long without going a little stir-crazy, Jace discovered after a couple of days. The scorching tropical sun made it unwise to spend too much time outside, though his winter-pale skin was already starting to develop a little golden color.

He'd developed a routine: he swam in the villa's private pool every morning, lay in the sun for a little while to dry off, then went inside and made breakfast. The villa's kitchen was as well-stocked as Luke had promised; he had no need to go anywhere.

Bored after the first half-day, he'd tried to log onto his email and do some work… only to find a single message from his father, advising him the IT wizards had locked him out of all company business until further notice. He was restricted to entertaining himself with the villa's well-stocked supply of books or laying on the couch catching up on *House Of Cards*.

Switching the TV off, Jace got up to pace the room restlessly. His energy levels were starting to return, and the unaccustomed inactivity was beginning to chafe. He should have put a gym in the villa, he thought grumpily. Not that he was in any fit state for his usual five-mile run on the treadmill.

Well, if he couldn't run, he could at least get outside for some fresh air. He'd go for a walk, and if he found he had the energy, he might go all the way to the main resort building and catch up with Luke.

Decision made, it was only a few minutes before he was outside, hat on his head to shield him from the sun and running shoes on his feet. Someone had left a map of the island on the hall table, with the walking trails clearly marked. He grabbed it on the way out and checked the best route to take. Across the middle of the island into the southern end of the resort, he decided. The map's key indicated it should take about twenty minutes to hike the trail.

Ten minutes later, as he finally reached the top of the trail, he had to stop and lean against a tree for a while to rest. *Should have brought water,* he reproached himself. *Stupid thing to forget.* He should have known better, but it had been several years since he'd been on a hike and he'd been too eager to get out of the house.

Jace examined the resort below him. There was a cluster of private cabins at this end and a pool with a bar, one of several restaurants, a little further away. He could get a drink at the pool bar; he'd at least had enough sense to shove the comp card Luke had given him into his pocket. Wiping sweat from his brow with the hem of his shirt and cursing his physical weakness under his breath for the umpteenth time, he started down the slope.

"One dirty martini." Nessa set the drink down in front of her customer, swiped the card through her reader, and offered it for his signature. Over his shoulder, she spied a man emerging from the rarely-used trailhead beyond the pool; he looked hot and sweaty. Shaking her head, she turned to rinse out her cocktail shaker. *That guy was sure gonna need a drink.*

Turning back just as he sat down on a bar stool, she slid a coaster in front of him and said, "Good afternoon. What can I get you?"

Light blue eyes blinked at her, and the man said, "You're English!"

"I'm *from* England. I'm an Australian citizen," she gave her usual response. "Been here nearly ten years now."

"I guess the accent never really goes away."

She smiled tightly, knowing her accent gave her away as being from one of the seedier parts of East London. "Indeed." Slapping a cocktail menu down before him with perhaps a little more force than actually necessary, she turned away to serve another customer who'd just swum up to the pool side of the bar.

When she returned, the man asked for something long and cooling. Tempted to pour him some iced water, she asked instead, "Virgin?"

Jace blinked in surprise. "It's been a while, but no, I'm not."

The bartender threw her head back and laughed. She was pretty, Jace had noticed that right off: her skin a rich dark bronze with black hair falling to her waist in a mass of tiny braids. When she laughed, she was really beautiful, dimples appearing in her cheeks, light amber-brown eyes flashing with mirth.

"I was asking if you want a hard or a soft drink. Alcoholic, or not," she said through girlish giggles.

"Oh." Abashed, he felt color coming to his face. "Sorry. Brain fog. I think I'm a bit overheated."

A tall glass of iced water was set in front of him. "Why don't you start with that, and then you can decide if you'd like something a bit stronger?" The dimples flashed again as she gave him a warm smile.

"Thank you… Nessa," he read the name tag on her blouse. "Short for Vanessa?"

"No."

"How interesting, your dimples disappear when your smile isn't genuine. Is it something embarrassing, then?"

Nessa's jaw dropped. "Are you always this direct?"

"I like to cut through the bullshit. Jace." He offered a hand across the bar. "Not short for anything. My mother just liked the name." Only after he'd already said it, did he think maybe he should have used a different first name. *Jace* wasn't exactly common, after all.

Nessa hesitated a minute, and then she took his hand, leaned forward, and whispered close to his ear, "Tennessee."

He grinned. "Nessa's better. Suits you. The other, I think I'd expect you to have a Southern drawl."

By now, Jace was the only one sitting at the bar. Nessa turned away from him, plucking a couple of bottles off the shelf. "No Southern drawl. I make a mean Georgia Peach, though."

She deftly poured peach schnapps, vodka, grenadine, and cranberry juice into a shaker with crushed ice, shook it up swiftly, and poured it into a tall glass, topping it off with lemonade and a maraschino cherry speared on a tiny plastic sword. "Give that a try."

His water glass was empty, Jace realized as she swept it from in front of him and replaced it with the cocktail. He didn't even remember draining it.

"Thanks." He took a sip, sighing with pleasure as the tart but sweet taste exploded over his tongue. "Ohhh. Oh, that's perfection."

Nessa smiled, turning to rinse her shaker out. "You're welcome. Got your card there?"

"Sure." He fished it out of his pocket, sliding it across the bar as she returned with a card reader.

Nessa swiped the card without looking at it, blinking as the reader immediately gave her a green light. "What--oh, this is a comp card." She handed it back with a curious look. "Are you staying at the main resort?"

"No, in one of the villas. It belongs to a friend." Jace took another long drink. "This really is exactly what I wanted. How did you know?"

"I'm psychic. Every good bartender is, don't ya know." Nessa flashed him a grin.

"I've heard that before. Half the ones I met in New York seemed to be studying psychiatry or psychology; they were pretty good mind-readers."

Nessa's smile was rather wry. "Psychiatry. Got my doctorate three years ago."

"Really?" He blinked at her. "Uh…"

"You're wondering why I'm still tending bar rather than earning a fortune in practice somewhere, right? I don't need to be a mind-reader to figure that one out. Almost everyone who knows I've got my doctorate has asked me the question at some point."

"Well, yeah." She was as sharp as she was beautiful, Jace found himself thinking, propping his elbows on the bar and listening in fascination as she spoke.

"I practiced for a year and realized I'd made a huge mistake." Nessa shrugged, leaning back against one of the low refrigerators behind her, arms folded over her chest. "Being responsible for other people's mental health is a massive burden, and one I was never really ready to take on."

"You lost a patient?" Jace guessed astutely.

"I lost a whole bunch of them. I was the junior staff psychiatrist at Wacol detention center in Brisbane. There was a prison riot." Nessa's eyes went dark and distant. "Four dead, all patients I'd seen in the previous month. Five more transferred to maximum security jails elsewhere."

"I'm sorry," Jace said quietly, knowing the sentiment was inadequate. Knowing she'd always blame herself, wonder if she could have seen it coming, could have done something to prevent it. "That must have been very difficult."

"As far as I was concerned, it was career-ending." Nessa picked up a clean glass and a cloth, and started polishing it unnecessarily. "I could have gone back, but I didn't want to. I tended bar throughout my degree and honestly I loved it. I went back to it permanently and decided to make it my career for good. Luke headhunted me for the resort about a year ago, and I never want to leave." She set the glass back into the rack of clean ones with a small smile. "So now I just dispense gentle advice and excellent drinks to people who are usually trying to relax anyway."

"I'll drink to that." Jace lifted his near-empty glass to her, thinking as he did so he almost envied Nessa her confidence, her surety she was now on the right path, even if it might not be the one she'd directed so much of her life to following. "Can I buy you one?" he offered on impulse.

"Thank you, but I don't drink on duty and I'm comped as much free soda as I can drink." Nessa shook her head at him with a smile, wondering as she did so why she'd told him so much of her story. She didn't usually open up to people this way on first meeting. There was something about Jace, though, something in his light blue eyes which made her think he would be a difficult person to lie to. "Another one of those?" She nodded at his glass.

"Better not, I haven't eaten for a few hours and I haven't had alcohol in a few weeks. I'll be all over the place."

"Drying out?"

"I've been ill, actually. Pneumonia."

Nessa nodded. She'd suspected something of the sort from the way his clothes hung a little on his frame, the gauntness of his cheeks, and the sallow tint to his skin. "Sunfish is a great place for recovery," she said. "Warm weather, great atmosphere. You staying long?"

Jace didn't detect any nosiness in the question; just natural curiosity. "Couple weeks, probably," he replied. "Maybe I'll see you around again."

"I'll be here." She tossed him a smile. "This is my bar. Eleven 'til seven, every day."

"You don't get any days off?" That didn't seem right. He'd have to speak to Luke about that; the staff needed personal time--

"Of course I do. It varies which ones, though. Depends on when I can get someone to cover."

"I see." He played with his empty glass, picking up the cherry and eating it before some impulse made him say, "Since you finish at seven, would you maybe care to have dinner with me?"

Nessa paused, her always-busy hands stilling on the glasses she'd been sorting. "Staff members aren't allowed to fraternize with resort guests."

"Fair enough, but I'm not technically a resort guest, am I? I'm staying in one of the villas."

She hesitated, then shook her head. "I have plans with some friends tonight."

Jace smiled, not taking offense. "Maybe another night."

"Maybe." She tipped her head noncommittally.

"It's been nice chatting with you, Nessa." He stood, stretched his arms up toward the sky with a sigh. "Oof, been too long since I did any exercise. I'm stiff just from that walk."

"Are you planning to walk back? Because it's gonna be dark soon, and we're up in the tropics here, we don't really get a twilight period. It goes from full light to pitch dark very fast."

"I've noticed that, watching the sunsets the last couple of days," Jace agreed with a nod.

"You don't want to be out on that trail in the dark. You won't be able to see your footing, might take a nasty fall…"

"You worried about me?" He gave her a cheeky smile. "Don't worry. I was planning on walking up to the main resort to see a friend who works there. I'll see if I can get him to give me a ride back in one of the golf carts."

"That sounds like a good plan." Nessa found herself watching as Jace stretched again, the hem of his T-shirt riding up to reveal a flat, toned stomach… was that actually a six-pack? He was an attractive man, she thought a little unwillingly, even with shaggy hair and a scruffy beard. She liked her men a little more clean-cut normally, but there was definitely something about Jace. Maybe it was those hypnotic light blue eyes. "See you again sometime."

"I certainly hope so." He gave her another broad smile before turning and heading off toward the main resort.

Nessa watched him until he was out of sight, wondering if she would indeed see him again. She didn't shake herself out of her reverie until a customer sat down at the bar and coughed politely to attract her attention.

CHAPTER TWO

Jace ambled toward the main resort, taking his time to look at the beautiful surroundings, the immaculately tended gardens. The private cabins placed discreetly away from the path looked inviting; he thought he would rather enjoy one of those, maybe more so than the large, empty villa he was rattling around in at the moment. It hadn't exactly been designed for one person.

Smiling at his own foolishness, he strolled on, his mind back on the woman he'd just met. Nessa was an intriguing, beautiful puzzle; he found himself disappointed she'd declined his dinner invitation, and not just because he was lonely for any company. She interested him far more than the women he usually met, glossy, corporate ladder-climbers in New York who seemed more interested in his position and connections than in him as a human. Nessa seemed *real*; her honesty about her past only made him curious to know more.

Of course, her beauty didn't hurt either, he acknowledged to himself as he walked up the white marble steps into the main resort.

Whatever genetic mixture had produced Nessa, it had gifted her with the kind of traffic-stopping looks which would probably have made her a successful catwalk model if she were about eight inches taller. Her face was imprinted in his memory: those wide, light-amber eyes, high cheekbones and delicately pointed chin, full soft lips curved into a knowing little smile.

"Shake it off," Jace told himself firmly. "She turned you down. She probably gets hit on twenty times a day, with a face like that." He'd stop by another afternoon and say hi, maybe gently repeat the offer, and if she said no again, he'd accept gracefully and shut his mouth. Pursuing a woman who didn't want to be chased was a dick move, and it wasn't like he ever lacked for feminine attention. With his looks and money…

Jace snorted, chuckling at himself. The last thing he wanted Nessa to be was the kind of woman who'd be interested in his money. How would she know he had any, besides? And as for looks… he raised his hand, ruefully running it over his scraggly beard. If he wanted to impress Nessa with those, he was going to need to clean up some.

Entering the main reception, he paused for a moment to admire the glass-domed atrium, the shimmering marble floor, and the huge tank of tropical fish opposite the reception desk. Hunter Enterprises had spent millions of dollars on Sunfish Island, and the money showed. The main building was magnificent, beautiful architecture and artistic design everywhere the eye settled.

Approaching the reception dress, he returned the friendly smile of the young man who greeted him. "I'm looking for Luke Collyer's office?"

"First floor, sir." The man pointed down the marble hall. "Just take the stairs and turn left at the top."

"Thank you." Jace followed the directions and found a glass-walled office with RESORT MANAGEMENT etched on the door. Inside, a young woman was shouldering her bag and heading out.

"Oh, hello!" She blinked in surprise as she almost collided with Jace. "Can I help you?"

"I was looking for Luke, but he probably already finished for the day. Never mind, I guess."

Blue eyes scanned his face, then the girl smiled. "You must be the friend Luke said might stop by. Jay, wasn't it? You can go on in. Maybe you can get him to finish work at a reasonable time, for once."

Jace didn't bother correcting her, just thanking her as she gestured him toward the inner office. Rapping on the door, he pushed it open and leaned in, grinning.

"Hey, your boss says you're working too hard."

Luke looked up from the computer screen he was frowning at, a smile coming to his face. "I was about to say that I'm the boss here, but technically I guess you do outrank me."

"I know I promised not to interfere in resort business," Jace said, moving fully into the room, "but it's come to my attention that my resort manager is working too hard, and you know what they say about someone who's all work and no play."

"You calling me dull?" Luke pushed his chair back, rose to his feet, and grinned broadly. "I'll show you dull. Come on. Time you sampled some of Sunfish Island's nightlife!"

"Be gentle with me," Jace begged laughingly as Luke slung his arm around Jace's shoulders and steered him out of the office. "I'm an invalid!"

They ended up in the resort's famous French restaurant. Recently awarded a Michelin star, the food was as good as anything Jace had eaten in the most expensive restaurants in New York. Luke called the sommelier over and ordered a bottle of an Australian white wine Jace hadn't heard of, which turned out to be so good Jace immediately decided to send his father a case.

"Damn," Jace said finally, sitting back in his seat and rubbing his stomach. "I don't think I'll have much trouble regaining the weight I've lost if I eat here regularly."

Luke chuckled, raising his glass to toast the sentiment. "I go running on the beach every morning to make sure I don't get tubby. The resort is extremely lucky to have Suzannah Monteil… I need to go through the budget and look at getting her another raise, actually, or she's gonna get poached from under our noses."

"I'll authorize it," Jace said immediately. "Pay her whatever you think fit. Word is going to get out pretty quickly and people will come to the resort just for the opportunity to eat here." He looked around the restaurant. He could only see one vacant table, a waitress already clearing and re-setting it to make it ready for occupation again. "It's already busy, but we could be completely booked out every night. A waiting list. Folks flying in by helicopter just to dine here."

"You sound like our marketing manager," Luke said with a grin. "I've already heard all this from her. I think she's got every major restaurant critic in the southern hemisphere lined up to visit us over the next month. That Michelin star has really put us on the map."

"Which is why you need to keep the chef no matter what." Jace nodded, his quick mind turning over the issue. "Is there any other incentive you want to offer her? Anything else she'd like?"

"I haven't really had the chance to sit down and talk with her about it." Luke shrugged. "Maybe you can meet with her yourself."

"I'll think about it, toward the end of my stay. I'd rather not talk to anyone in my official persona before that. Keep it quiet that I'm here, please."

Luke nodded. "Sure."

"You have my complete support in offering her whatever the hell she wants to get her to agree to stay, though," Jace offered. "Up to and including moving into the family villa once I've gone, if she'd care for more luxurious living quarters."

That made Luke laugh. "I'll keep that card up my sleeve just in case. I very much doubt she'd accept, though. Suzannah is… well, she's not the sort to be tempted by money or luxuries. Honestly, she'll probably demand the authority to order loads more exotic ingredients for the restaurant."

"Fine by me," Jace said, "she'll probably earn us another Michelin star with them, so authorize away." He toasted Luke with the last of the wine before draining it. "Hey, do I need to run the comp card?"

Luke waved him away. "It's all taken care of, don't worry. You had enough? Want a coffee?"

"Honestly, I'm fighting to keep my eyelids open," Jace confessed. "The rest of that nightlife you promised me might have to wait for another day."

"It's all good, mate." Luke gave him a warm smile. "You look pretty done in. Let me run you back home, eh? Get some rest. I don't want to be the cause of a relapse; your father would kill me!"

Jace found his head nodding as Luke drove the golf cart back to the villa. "Is it okay if I wander over again tomorrow?" he asked drowsily. "I could stop by and see Nessa again."

"Oh, you met Nessa?" Luke glanced at him as he pulled the cart to a stop. "She's something, isn't she? A real asset for the resort. I ran across her slinging drinks in a bar near the football ground in Brisbane; I'd never seen anyone make cocktails so fast."

The mental image made Jace smile as he got out of the cart and thanked Luke for the ride and his company at dinner. Luke sped off with a cheerful wave and Jace let himself into the villa, collapsing to lie on the couch. He fell asleep right there, worn out from the unaccustomed exercise, delicious food, and the alcohol he'd consumed.

*   *   *

Jace woke with a dry mouth, a sore head, and a desperate need to visit the bathroom. Attending to the last need first, he found some painkillers in his toiletries bag and washed them down with a large glass of water. A couple of slices of toast and three more glasses of water later, he started to feel a little more human. *No more drinking with Luke*, he concluded. The aftermath was no fun.

Refilling his glass again, he took it outside and sat by the villa's pool, dangling his feet in the sparkling blue water and gazing out over the pool's infinity edge at the ocean.

"I could live here," he said aloud, startling himself with the revelation. For years, his view had been the New York City skyline from his penthouse apartment; before that it was Sydney. Both cities with spectacular views available to anyone who cared to look. Still, this place had that one thing both places would never have: tranquility.

It was something Jace had never realized was missing from his life, until yesterday. The knowledge the phone wasn't going to ring, that nobody would bother him unless he actively went out and sought company, was eye-opening. For the first time he could remember, there were literally no demands on his time at all.

He'd thought the forced inactivity and solitude would drive him crazy with boredom. Instead, he seemed to have unlocked something which had been stagnant for too long: his creativity. Ideas for designs were beginning to surface in his head, as they hadn't since he gave up his dreams of being a full-time architect and joined Hunter Enterprises at his father's behest.

Nessa's story popped back into his head: the way she'd told him so emphatically she never wanted to leave Sunfish, despite her qualifications for a much more high-powered job. She'd consciously chosen a simpler life and found contentment. Perhaps it was her words which caused his introspection now, making him reconsider his own life choices. Kicking his feet absently in the water and watching the ripples spread out from the movement, Jace sighed. He couldn't walk away from his responsibilities, tempting though the idea seemed. His father had been grooming him for years to take over Hunter Enterprises, and Jace had excelled in every role he'd been given.

Capability did not equal enjoyment, however, and Jace hadn't enjoyed the work in a while. For the first time, he began to consider alternatives. Maybe he could speak to his father about other options, about looking at someone else being Chief Executive when his father decided to step down, because the idea of being responsible for the whole shebang seemed completely unpalatable.

The sun felt hot on his back, and he didn't have sunscreen on. Pushing himself up, Jace dried his legs off and headed back inside. Maybe he'd check in with his father. Just say hi. A quick calculation told him it was early evening in New York, a pretty good time to call. John would probably still be at the office.

Jace had to convince his own assistant to put him through. Nancy was a dragon, but a wonderful one; she managed every aspect of his life and mothered him unmercifully when he let her get away with it. She flatly refused to put him through to his father until he promised he wouldn't talk business, that it was just a social call.

"How's the sun, sea, and sand?" John Hunter boomed down the phone, making Jace grin. His father was always a larger-than-life character.

"I haven't actually been in the sea yet."

"Why not? It's not jellyfish season, is it?"

"No." Jace chuckled. "I just haven't got around to it, honestly. The villa's got almost everything I need, I haven't wanted to leave. I went over to the resort yesterday, had dinner with Luke. Don't worry, though, he told me straight up he'd kick me out if I even tried to talk business."

"I know."

"Of course you do," Jace realized. "You've been checking up on me."

"Actually, I called Luke to congratulate him on the restaurant getting a Michelin star. He told me he saw you yesterday, and that you seemed well but still kinda tired." John's voice softened, gentled. "And if I *was* checking up on you, Jace, it'd only be because I'm worried about you. You gave me a damn scare."

"I know. I'm sorry, Dad."

"I never wanted you to run yourself into the ground, son. You don't have to prove anything to me. I'm already proud of you."

A lump welled in Jace's throat; he took a moment to clear it before he simply said, "Thanks."

"Everything is fine here without you. Frankly, I think Nancy could run the place perfectly well without either of us."

Jace grinned at that. "I don't doubt it. Hey," he said as something occurred to him, "you should take a break here too, Dad. How long is it since you've been on vacation?"

"Flew up for Hamilton Race Week last year," John answered promptly. "Might come up this year too. It's only a few weeks away now, I've got several friends with yachts in the races. Maybe you'll still be there?"

"I hope not. I'll go stir-crazy by then with nothing to do!"

John laughed richly. "Go find some pretty girls to flirt with or something."

Unbidden, Jace's mind flew to Nessa. "Maybe," he said unguardedly, then changed the subject before his father could ask any awkward questions.

Hanging up the phone at last, Jace found he felt almost light, as though a weight had been taken off his shoulders. The news Hunter Enterprises was ticking along just fine without him should have been a cause for concern, a worry he was replaceable. Instead, the knowledge was strangely reassuring. Was it a sign, he wondered? A sign maybe his future really didn't lie in the company's executive offices?

Well, he didn't have to make the decision today, or tomorrow, or even next week. He had plenty of time to consider it, and where better than here, in this island paradise, with nothing else to distract the mind? Dropping the phone on the coffee table, he lay back on the couch, putting his feet up, and gazed up at the ceiling. The sun reflecting off the pool outside made little ripples of dappled light on the white paint. Gazing at them, Jace's eyes slowly drifted closed until he was sound asleep.

CHAPTER THREE

Nessa hadn't expected to see Jace back at her bar, and certainly not so soon, but she was serving lunchtime drinks when he came ambling down off the hiking trail again. He looked a lot better today and better equipped as well, with a small pack slung over his shoulder. She guessed he had a water bottle in it. Too busy to do more than give him a quick nod in greeting as he slid onto a barstool, she took a few minutes to clear the order the waiter had just handed her for a dozen complicated cocktails.

"Hey," she slid a coaster in front of Jace and smiled. "You look better today. Got some color in your cheeks."

He smiled back. "I totally had a grandpa nap after breakfast. It was fantastic."

That made Nessa laugh. "Good for you. What can I get you?"

"Haven't had lunch yet, so I'd better keep it virgin." He cocked his head at her. "Something long and cold. I brought water with me today, but it's still pretty hot walking."

She nodded and reached for a tall glass, shoveling ice into it before mixing orange, mango, and pineapple juices and topping it off with club soda.

"Looks great," Jace said enthusiastically as Nessa placed the glass in front of him with a flourish. He took a long drink, eyes closing with pleasure. "Ohhh. Beautiful."

"You're welcome." She set one of the food menus down beside his glass. "If you want to order lunch, I can put your order through here and the kitchen will send it out shortly."

"Oh, you do bar food here?" He picked up the menu and looked through it with interest, seeing a wide variety of dishes, from pizza and sandwiches to Asian dishes and Spanish tapas.

"One of the resort's restaurants is right over there," she gestured to a large hedge to one side of the pool. "The kitchen's just behind the bar. You can go in there for lunch, if you'd prefer."

"No, I think I'd like to eat here," Jace said thoughtfully. "Turkey and cheese focaccia with cranberry sauce sounds good, please."

Nessa put the order through, poured two more drinks as her waiter returned, and then found herself leaning with her elbows on the bar. "Have you been here on Sunfish long?"

"A few days, but I didn't really venture out until yesterday." He smiled at her. "I'm planning to remedy that, though, and do some exploring. This place really is like paradise."

Nessa smiled as she looked around, at the laughing patrons in the shimmering pool, the beautifully landscaped tropical gardens. "It really is. I get a bit blasé about it sometimes, but then someone like you comes along and makes me look at it through fresh eyes."

Jace nodded, taking another sip of his drink.

"Do you snorkel, or dive?" Nessa asked then. "If so, you should, while you're here. We're right in the middle of the World Heritage part of the Barrier Reef; there's no better diving anywhere in the world."

"I haven't for a long time, but I'd love to." He hesitated, remembering her quick refusal of his invitation the previous afternoon. "Do you get much chance to?"

"I haven't been in ages." She looked a bit wistful. "I really should. It's still fairly quiet this time of year, I could get a spot on one of the trips easily enough. In the high season, we're supposed to leave them for paying customers, obviously."

"Obviously," Jace agreed, nodding. It was a sensible policy. He fiddled with the straw in his drink for a moment. *Go on, bite the bullet. The worst she can say is no.* "I was thinking of maybe going up to the main resort and booking onto one of the trips. If you've got a day off coming up, maybe you'd like to come with me?"

He hadn't felt so shy asking a girl out in years. Nessa's light amber eyes were serious as she gazed at him, and then her dimpled smile broke out, wide and startlingly white in her brown face.

"I'd really like that. I've got the day off tomorrow, actually, if there are any spots available on one of the tours."

Jace had to suppress an inappropriate urge to punch the sky and whoop with victory. *Play it cool.* "Any preferences, snorkel or dive?"

"Snorkel. I've never been much of a diver, I admit. I get a bit claustrophobic."

He nodded, perfectly happy with that. "Sounds good. I'll walk over after lunch and check out what's available."

Nessa smiled and turned away to serve another customer. She couldn't keep her lips from quirking upward, she found; the thought of going snorkeling with Jace had a squirmy, excited feeling building in the pit of her stomach. *It's a date,* she thought, giving him a quick sideways glance under her lashes. His sandwich had just been delivered and he was thanking the waitress who'd brought it with a charming smile. The girl looked a bit dazed as she turned away; she caught Nessa's eye and grinned, miming fanning herself with a backward glance at Jace.

He's sexy enough to raise any girl's internal temperature, Nessa thought. Add his physical attractiveness, charm, and money—at least, she assumed he was reasonably well off. Enough to move in the rarefied circles where a friend owned a private villa on Sunfish Island, at any rate. Although she supposed it could be a friend with rich parents; there weren't many folks Jace's age who had that kind of money.

Everything about Jace added up to the kind of man women threw themselves at. And he'd chosen to ask her out, not once but twice, making a second attempt when she'd turned him down the first time. It was flattering as hell, Nessa acknowledged, glancing at him again, taking in his clean-cut, preppy good looks. He'd shaved since yesterday, removing the scraggly beard, and though he could still use a haircut, he looked even more handsome than she'd originally thought.

She was still busy serving customers when he finished eating and headed off, though he did catch her eye to give her a little wave. Her heart sank unaccountably, but leapt right back up again twenty minutes later when he ambled back to the bar, waving a slip of paper.

"We're booked on the all-day snorkel tour going out at eight-thirty," Jace said cheerfully as Nessa gave him one of her blinding smiles.

"Sounds terrific. I'll meet you at the dock?"

"Sure. They said the boat is equipped with everything we need, so all you need to bring is your beautiful self and your swim gear."

"You'd better wear a T-shirt." She pointed at him. "And we'll slather you in sunscreen, or that pasty skin of yours is gonna go lobster-red."

"Gotcha," Jace agreed. "Well, I'd better head on back. See you in the morning, then!"

"See you," Nessa said, and told herself not to be silly. It was ridiculous to be disappointed he hadn't repeated his dinner invitation. She'd be spending the whole day with him tomorrow. That'd be plenty of time to get to know him better.

*   *   *

Nessa woke early the following morning. Butterflies churned in her stomach. She told herself sternly not to be ridiculous; she was hardly a teenager on her first date with a boy she liked! Still, she couldn't quite tamp down the welling bubble of excitement as she headed to the staff cafeteria to get breakfast.

"Hey!" Her friend Olivia slid into the seat opposite her. "You're up and about early. Don't usually see you in here at this hour."

"I'm going out on a snorkeling trip today," Nessa explained. "Figured I should get in a good breakfast first; I'll need the energy."

Olivia shuddered dramatically. "You don't get seasick? I never dare eat if I'm going out on one of the boats, in case I wind up feeding the fish!"

"…Thanks for that image." Nessa looked down at the stack of waffles she'd selected, having second thoughts.

"Whoops, never mind me!" Olivia laughed, a blush staining her cheeks. "Shouldn't have

160

mentioned it. You just have a good day!" Nessa couldn't keep the goofy grin off her face, and Olivia gave her a narrow-eyed look. "Why do I have the feeling this isn't just a fun day off for you? Wait. You met someone!"

"What are you, a mind-reader?" Nessa dug back into her waffles. "Yes, I met someone," she mumbled when Olivia prodded her.

"A resort guest?" Olivia's eyes widened.

"No! Come on, you know me better than that. He's staying at one of the private villas. It belongs to a friend of his."

"Oh, okay." Olivia nodded. "Is he cute?" Her grin widened cheekily.

"Well, I think so." Nessa grinned back. "But paws off. You're taken." She pointed her fork at Olivia sternly.

"Oh, don't worry, I'm more than satisfied with my catch." Olivia looked like a cat licking cream off her whiskers.

"And where is Cory this morning?" she asked, referring to the resort's activities manager.

"Oh, he's taking the snorkeling trip out. He already ate and went down to help prep the boat. So don't tell me, if you don't want to, but be warned I'll get all the juicy details out of Cory later. Can't escape the gossip network, darling."

Nessa wrinkled her nose with disgust and sighed. "Well, it's a first date. So there won't be much to tell."

"Apart from the fact that your date will no doubt be eating you up with his eyes. Are you wearing your red bikini? You'll knock his socks off."

She already had it on underneath her light sundress. Living on a tropical island, she owned half a dozen bikinis, but she never considered wearing any of the others when she opened the drawer this morning. The red bikini was a halter-neck, framing and lifting her breasts, the fiery color a great contrast to her dark skin. Ties at the sides of the brief bikini bottoms were a wicked temptation, luring a man's attention to her hips, making him think about tugging on the ties to pull them free.

Nessa wanted that kind of attention from Jace. She'd done a fair bit of soul-searching after impulsively agreeing to go on the snorkeling date with him. She wasn't an impulsive person by nature, but in the end she'd had to conclude her subconscious had already decided. Jace was an attractive man. He wasn't the only one to show interest in her recently, but he was the only one in a long time who'd provoked a matching response from her. She'd spend the day with him and see how things panned out, but at the moment she provisionally intended on taking him back to her place that evening. Or going back to the villa where he was staying, if he invited her. She'd never been in any of the fancy private villas and found herself curious about what they'd be like.

"Earth to Nessa!"

She blinked, startled back to herself. She'd drifted off into a daydream thinking about Jace. About letting him pull the ties on her bikini. He had nice hands, she'd noticed when he was at the bar, with long, capable fingers. She'd had more than a few thoughts about those fingers caressing her skin, finding her most sensitive spots.

"Sorry, I was somewhere else."

"I could see that." Olivia smirked over the rim of her coffee cup. "You'd better get moving, sugar, or you're literally gonna miss that boat."

"Argh!" A quick glance at her watch and Nessa abandoned the remnants of her breakfast, scrabbling under her chair for the beach bag she'd brought with her.

"Have fun!" Olivia called after her as she hurried for the exit. Nessa waved hastily and set off for the boat dock at a fast trot.

CHAPTER FOUR

She wasn't coming. It was eight twenty-eight, and the boathand was preparing to cast off the lines. Jace bit down on his lip, wondering if he could ask them to wait five more minutes.

"We're one short," the tall blond man in resort-uniform polo shirt and shorts said, looking at the clipboard in his hand. "You're Jace Weller, right?"

He'd given his mother's maiden name as his surname when booking, not wanting anyone to clue in to his real identity. "That's right."

"And you booked for two?"

"Yeah, my friend should be here any minute--" He spied a figure hurrying along the path toward the dock. "Here she is now!"

"Hold off on that line, Ben." The man took a half a step back. "Whoa, Nessa?"

"Hey, Cory," Nessa grinned at him as she hurried up to the boat. "Hi, Jace." To his pleased surprise, she went up on tiptoes and brushed a kiss on his cheek.

"I... see." Cory blinked, looking from one to the other of them. "Okay, well, I guess that makes everyone, then." He made a final tick on his clipboard. "Take your seats, everyone."

There were several other guests on board and only a couple of seats vacant. Nessa sat down and Jace joined her; she dropped a bag at their feet and gave him a bright smile.

"You look beautiful," Jace said impulsively. She was wearing a light cotton sundress in a turquoise blue which looked utterly amazing against her deep brown skin. Her long black braids were hanging loose to her waist, brushing against his arm; he suppressed an inappropriate urge to take one in his fingers and play with it.

"Thank you!" Nessa held his gaze, her smile widening even further. "You're looking pretty good yourself. Like the threads." She flicked lightly at the lapel of the loud Hawaiian shirt he was wearing.

"It's not mine," Jace confessed, "I think it belongs to… the owner of the villa. I found it in the closet." He'd almost said *my father* then, but bit the words back just in time. He'd told Nessa the villa belonged to a friend. An uncomfortable feeling curled in the pit of his stomach; he didn't like misleading her. But then, he rationalized, he wanted her to get to know him without knowing who he was, about his wealth, his family name. It was very possible nothing would come of this, that they would go their separate ways in a few days and she would never even need to know.

Still, as he looked into her smiling, carefree face, Jace had the sinking feeling things weren't going to be quite so simple.

A heavy hand landed on his shoulder, making him jump. The boat had started moving, and he twisted around to find Cory had slipped into the seat behind them and was giving him the evil eye.

"Knock it off with the big brother act, Cory," Nessa said, shoving Cory's hand off Jace's shoulder. "I'm a big girl, y'know."

"Just making sure he knows there are folks looking out for you," Cory said, his tone perfectly amiable even if his eyes weren't.

"I had no doubt of it," Jace said with a friendly smile in return. "I'm sure Nessa's the kind of person who inspires intense loyalty in her friends."

Cory nodded, apparently satisfied with his answer. "Good. Well, in that case, have a good day!" He slid out of the seat again and strode up to the front of the boat, easily maintaining his footing against the sway, plucking up a microphone from the side of the pilot's chair. "G'day folks! Let me tell you about the awesome day we've got in store for you…"

Jace and Nessa both listened with interest as Cory talked, telling the group the itinerary for the day, including snorkeling at three different sites and lunch on the world-famous Whitehaven Beach.

"With any luck we'll see some humpback whales too, since they're passing through the area at the moment on their annual migration," Cory concluded, "so keep your eyes peeled."

The other tourists started chattering excitedly as soon as Cory put the microphone down. Nessa looked at Jace, her eyes shining. "I'm really looking forward to this. Thank you so much for inviting me."

"I'm looking forward to it too. The snorkeling… and your company."

Small fingers curled over his. Startled, Jace looked down at Nessa's hand, then up at her. She was still smiling at him. He turned his hand and laced his fingers with hers, feeling like a boy with his first crush finding out the girl he liked was interested in him, too.

They held hands the whole half-hour it took to get to the first snorkeling site, a secluded cove in the lee of one of the other islands in the chain. Cory informed them the island was completely uninhabited, a wildlife sanctuary, and they weren't permitted to swim ashore.

Jace had shoved his bag under the seat when he'd boarded. He pulled it out now and stripped off his Hawaiian shirt. Catching Nessa eying his chest, he grinned at her. He was picking up some color to his skin after a few days relaxing by the villa's pool, and though he was still thinner than he'd been before his illness, it only threw his muscles into higher relief.

"I could leave the rash vest off if you want to admire the view," he offered, the stretchy swim shirt hanging from one hand.

Nessa laughed at him. "Put it on. I don't want to be distracted from the sights underwater." She rose to her feet, grasped the hem of her dress, and swept it up and over her head in one graceful movement.

Jace almost swallowed his tongue. "You think *you'll* get distracted?"

Nessa grinned, walking past him to scoop up a pair of flippers and a snorkel mask from the stack Cory had spread out on the deck. "Hurry up. No time to waste!"

Jace was all fingers and thumbs trying to get his rash vest on, then grabbing a mask and flippers. Cory laughed at him as he hopped on one foot, trying to wrestle a flipper on.

"She's right there, man. Wow, you've got it bad, huh?"

"Are you dead? Did you see her in that bikini?"

"Not dead, just very happily taken." Cory grinned at him before reverting to business mode. "Remember, don't touch any of the coral. You want to climb down the ladder?"

Jace shook his head. "I'm good. I'm a strong swimmer." Checking nobody was directly beneath him, he fitted his mask and snorkel before diving smoothly off the back of the boat.

Nessa wasn't far away, floating face-down on the surface of the water in a deadman's float position, obviously looking at something beneath the surface. Jace swam up beside her, swishing his flippers gently, peering into the clear blue water to see what she was looking at.

Nessa turned her head slightly to look at him without taking her face out of the water, reaching to touch his wrist lightly before pointing.

It took Jace a moment to see what she was gesturing at; she appeared to be telling him to look at a surprisingly plain patch of sand in the midst of some bright corals. Frowning, he peered closer, but then the sand shifted and he gasped, almost losing the rhythm of his breathing through the snorkel, as a stingray almost as long as he was lifted up out of the sand and sailed majestically off into the blue.

Jace looked at Nessa, eyes wide, sensing rather than seeing her amusement at his shock.

She touched his wrist again before swishing her flippers to move on.

They surfaced for a proper breath a few minutes later and Jace spat to clear his mouth of the salty water. "My God, that was incredible! Did you see the size of that stingray?"

"A spotted eagle ray, I think," Nessa said, laughing at his excited expression. "You'll have to meet our marine biologists sometime."

Jace nodded. A large part of the reason Hunter Enterprises had been allowed to redevelop Sunfish Island had been the huge marine biology research and education facility they'd agreed to build and permanently fund. One of the finest of its kind in the world, it had a team of four permanent research scientists and half a dozen assistants who came up on funded semester-long assignments from universities across Australia. Parts of the facility were open the the public; he'd been meaning to visit but hadn't had the opportunity yet. "I'd love to."

"I'll take you," Nessa said impulsively. "Laurie, one of the marine biologists, is a friend of mine. She'll take you on a behind-the-scenes tour if you're with me."

It was on the tip of his tongue to tell her it wasn't necessary, that Luke could arrange things, but he rethought the impulse. Nessa would want to know why Luke would be so willing to accommodate him, and that opened him up to questions he wasn't ready to answer. Besides, Nessa taking him to the facility would definitely be a second date.

"Thanks," he said, "that would be awesome."

"We could go early, before I start work. I'll catch up with her tomorrow and find out what day would suit." Nessa was bubbling with excitement, too. She pulled her snorkel down to her mouth again. "Come on. I want to see if we can spot any clown fish!"

Grinning, Jace popped his mouthpiece back in and dived after her.

The water was warm and buoyant, and in the sheltered cove there was no current to speak of. It was like swimming through a warm bath, relaxing and easy. Everywhere Jace looked, there was something new and amazing to see: brightly colored corals, invertebrates, and fish. Nessa pointed out a starfish of such an intense blue, even underwater, Jace could hardly believe it was real. He swam on at her side, head turning every which way as he tried to take it all in.

A sharp whistle cut the air as he surfaced briefly to get a deep breath. Surprised, Jace checked his dive watch. Cory had told them they'd have fifty minutes at this stop. Startled to see their time was up, he reached out and tapped Nessa's shoulder, then his watch.

She nodded and pulled her mouthpiece out. "That went quickly!"

"Certainly did," he agreed, as they turned and began swimming back to the boat. They weren't too far away; they'd been careful to reorient themselves on the boat each time they surfaced, swimming tracks parallel to their previous courses.

Cory leaned down to give them both a hand up. Jace waited for Nessa to go first, completely failing to keep his eyes off her beautiful butt as she climbed back aboard the boat. But then, it would have been most ungallant of him to make her wait in the water while he got out, and it would have taken a lot more discipline than he possessed not to look.

She looked over her shoulder at him and laughed.

He shrugged unapologetically. "I'm not dead."

"Good thing, too." Cory offered his hand but Jace waved him off, climbing the ladder back into the boat easily. Sitting back down beside Nessa, he accepted the bottle of water she handed him from the large cooler in the middle of the boat's hull.

"You look a bit pale," she noted, her eyes searching his face. "Are you feeling alright?"

"Yep." He was grateful for the chance to sit down and rest, though, while the boat took them to their next location. Cursing the lingering weakness which still plagued his body after his illness, he cracked the top of the water and took a long drink.

"I brought snacks." Nessa delved into the bag at her feet. "Healthy--" she held up a small bunch of ripe bananas, "--or not so healthy." She waved a large bar of chocolate at him.

"Both?"

"Both is good. Fruit first?" Splitting a couple of bananas off the bunch, she handed one over. Jace peeled his and ate it with enjoyment, unable to keep his mind out of the gutter as he watched Nessa eat hers, her lips puckering around the fruit in an insanely erotic gesture. She knew exactly what she was doing to him, as well, her laughing eyes holding his as she ate.

Jace was glad his board shorts were loose.

*   *   *

Their second snorkeling location was at a platform anchored on an open-water coral reef. The water here was shallower than at the first site, so they just floated side by side, face down in the water, gazing with wonder at the natural beauties of the reef. Nessa got to see her clown fish and a couple of dozen other species besides.

"Next stop: Whitehaven Beach," Cory said as they climbed back aboard once again. "You ever been there, Jace?"

He shook his head. "Looking forward to seeing it."

"It's one of the most beautiful beaches in the world. Sand so white it looks like snow." Nessa sounded like a tourist brochure, not that he minded in the slightest. She practically glowed with happiness, her smile wide and white, her dark skin glimmering with salt water.

Tentatively, Jace slipped his arm around her waist as they sat back down, leaning over to kiss the point of her shoulder lightly.

Nessa's breath drew in softly as she looked at him. He'd been the perfect gentleman so far, gallant and charming, though his eyes had told a different story as he'd watched her. His lips were warm against her skin, his eyes questioning as he lifted his head to look at her.

Leaning in, Nessa put her hand to Jace's cheek and brought her lips to his. He closed his eyes, she saw in the instant before she closed her own.

The first kiss was light, little more than a gentle press of lips. Jace didn't push, didn't try to pull her closer, and his reticence made Nessa want more. She kissed him with greater fervor, her lips parting, tongue flicking between them to trace over the seam of his. Then, at last, he kissed her back properly. His arm tightened around her waist as his tongue danced with hers, and Nessa slid her hand into his damp blond hair, grasping the wet locks.

"Ahem," Cory's not-at-all-subtle cough brought them back to awareness of their surroundings.

Probably a good thing too, Nessa realized ruefully. She'd been just about to climb astride Jace's lap and grab his hands and bring them to her breasts. Her nipples were aching inside her wet bikini top, wanting stimulation. With a reluctant sigh, she pulled back from the kiss, giving Cory a glare.

In response, he flicked his eyes at a couple of giggling teenagers on the other side of the boat.

Cory was right; they didn't need to be getting hot and heavy in public. But Jace's kiss had woken something deep inside of Nessa which she'd kept dormant for a long time. The end of the boat trip seemed very far away, and Nessa hoped she'd be able to hold out until they could finally be alone together.

"We're coming up to Whitehaven Beach now," Cory announced. "You can have a swim or whatever while we're setting up lunch; it'll be ready in about fifteen minutes. We've got an hour and a half total here, so make the most of it!"

Nessa hesitated, then asked Cory quietly, "Do you want any help getting lunch set up?"

He smiled down at her, touching her shoulder. "Nah, hon, you're all good. You're a paying guest today, courtesy of Jace here. You just have fun. I do this three or four times a week, got it down to a fine art."

She gave him a grateful smile.

"Damn, that sand really is white," Jace said in amazement, shielding his eyes from the sun's reflected glare. "Is it coarse sand, or fine?"

"Incredibly fine, ike powdered sugar," Nessa remembered from her previous visit. "It gets *everywhere*."

"At least we'll be swimming again afterward. And hey, if it gets in your bikini, I'll volunteer to help you get it out." Jace grinned wickedly.

She elbowed him lightly in the ribs, grinning back. "Behave, or our chaperone will be telling us off again."

They were both giggling like kids as they climbed off the back of the boat into the shallow water and walked hand-in-hand to the beach. The fine powdery sand promptly coated their wet legs, as Nessa had warned.

"This looks a nice spot," Nessa said as they reached a secluded section of the beach. "You okay to lie in the sun for a bit?"

"Sure, I'll just put some more sunscreen on."

They both spread out towels and lay down. Nessa pointed at her lower legs, laughing. "Look, my legs are nearly as white as yours!"

"Nessa!" Jace chuckled. "Never say that. Your skin is beautiful."

"Please say you're not going to call me cocoa or chocolate or anything like that?" She rolled to her front, shading her eyes with her hand to look at him.

"Come on! I'm an Aussie but I've been working in New York for five years now. I know how culturally insensitive it is to compare skin tones to food." He gave her a reproving look. "I'm not much for flowery similes as compliments, anyway. Blatant honesty is more my thing."

"Blatant honesty?" Nessa crinkled her eyebrows.

"You're incredibly beautiful. Your skin glows. Your eyes sparkle. I find it very hard to look anywhere else when I'm with you."

"…Okay, that's pretty blatant," Nessa said when she got her breath back. "Wow."

Jace grinned at her. "Just making sure you know how I feel. I could go on, if you like?"

"My head might get too swollen and explode. You're very good for my ego, though."

He reached across the small gap between their towels, fingers curling gently around hers. "I'd like to be good for a lot of things for you, Nessa. Sneaking off into the undergrowth to make out like a pair of horny teenagers is sounding mighty appealing right about now."

"If it wasn't for the wildlife, which would no doubt make that into a very dangerous endeavor." Nessa grinned back at him.

"Come on, I'm an Aussie. Snakes and spiders don't terrify me."

"I'm a Brit, and they do bloody well terrify me! Besides, it's the lizards you've got to worry about. Cory told me he saw a five foot long goanna here a couple of weeks ago."

"They're not gonna attack you." Jace chuckled at her expression of horror.

"Thanks, but I'm not prepared to risk my toes for the sake of a make out session with you.

Tempting though that may be. You'll just have to wait until later."

"Later?" His fingers squeezed a little more firmly on hers.

Nessa smiled. "Later."

And with that answer, Jace had to be content, as Cory's sharp whistle called them up the beach for lunch.

CHAPTER FIVE

Nessa nudged Jace. "Wake up."

"Huh!" His eyes snapped open. "Whoa. I was pretty sound asleep, huh?" Yawning and stretching, he rubbed at the back of his head.

"I don't think the boat engine had even started before you were snoozing on my shoulder." She smiled at him. "You're still not fully recovered, huh?"

"Pneumonia really knocks the stuffing out of you," Jace admitted, "and it's been a pretty big day. Sorry. Didn't mean to drop off on you."

"It's fine!" She squeezed his hand lightly. "I wouldn't have woken you up, except we're almost home." She nodded forward, and he looked to see they were indeed slowing to move into Sunfish Island's dock.

"So we are." He hesitated a moment before saying, "Would you like to come back to the villa with me? I've got a fridge full of food, we can easily throw together something for dinner."

"Sounds lovely," Nessa said, enthusiasm clear in her tone.

Jace had taken the golf cart stored in the villa's small garage to get to the dock that morning. He gestured to it now as they disembarked and bid farewell to Cory. "I didn't think my legs would be up to walking back after a day spent swimming and snorkeling."

"My legs thank you for the consideration." Nessa tossed her bag into the back and settled into the plush leather passenger seat with a sigh of contentment. "And so does my butt; this is so much more comfy than those hard plastic seats on the boat!"

"Wait until you try out the showers at the villa." Jace grinned, getting in and starting the cart.

"Giant shower roses?"

"Yup, with super-high pressure. Not only that, they have adjustable jets coming at you from every direction."

Nessa moaned. "Drive faster."

"Yes, ma'am," Jace chuckled. "It's just up ahead."

"This one?" Nessa gaped as they approached and Jace pushed a button on the dash to open the garage door. "Wow, this is one of the best locations on the island!"

"Oh?" Jace said, deliberately obtuse.

"I've always loved the design of this house, too. Lucky you, to be friends with the owners," Nessa sighed enviously as they parked inside and got out of the golf cart. "Well, at least I get to be nosy and look around inside!"

"Poke your nose anywhere you like. I have free run of the place," Jace said, with absolute honesty.

Nessa gazed around admiringly as they entered the house proper, taking everything in: the high ceilings, the glass doors which slid all the way back to give an unobstructed view over the pool to the ocean, the imported Carrara marble tiles on the floor. Even the furniture looked architecturally designed, though still somehow temptingly comfortable. There were a few books and a laptop lying on the coffee table, but otherwise the place was very tidy and barely looked inhabited. Jace was obviously not a slob, she noted approvingly, as she glanced into the kitchen and saw no dirty dishes on the counter or in the sink.

"All the bedrooms have en suite bathrooms," Jace said. "There's one on this level and four upstairs."

Nessa didn't hesitate before saying, "Which one are you using?"

"The one on this level… too lazy to walk upstairs when I'm tired." He smiled self-deprecatingly. "You're welcome to use any of the others."

"Or I could share yours." Her eyes held his.

Jace drew a deep breath. "You're very welcome to share mine. Why don't you go have a shower while I quickly throw something together for dinner?"

"Sounds good," Nessa agreed, though she'd been rather hoping Jace might come shower with her. On the other hand, they were both sticky and sandy; a chance to wash up and eat first would be welcome.

"Right in here." He opened a door and showed her into a stunning bedroom suite, sharing the same magnificent views as the main room. The king-sized bed was made up with what Nessa guessed were silk sheets, in a stunning shade of turquoise blue. A door on the other side of the room opened into a lavishly appointed bathroom; plush towels in the same shade of turquoise hung on chrome towel racks on the wall. A third door led to a huge walk-in closet, with a few of Jace's things taking up scant space on the hangers and shelves.

"Wow," Nessa said, mouth open. She'd never seen a bedroom suite like this, and Jace had said the house had four more of them. "I guess this is how the other half live, huh?"

"Yeah." This was probably the most cheaply-appointed room Jace had occupied in the last five years; it was certainly nothing compared to his New York penthouse or the spectacular family mansion in Sydney's exclusive Point Piper. He was hardly going to mention that at the moment, though, so he took a step back. "I'll leave you to it. Make yourself comfortable."

She smiled at him as he backed out of the room, closing the door behind him.

Blowing out his cheeks, Jace headed for the kitchen. Pumping soap and washing his hands, he wondered what the hell he was doing. He didn't like misleading Nessa this way, pretending to be something he wasn't. On the other hand, he had the feeling Nessa would probably take off if she had any idea he took this kind of luxury for granted, that his family owned not only this house but the entire damned island.

With a sigh, he turned to the fridge. When Nessa came out, dressed again in her turquoise sundress, she found him chopping peppers and shallots, wielding an expensive chef's knife with flashing speed. He'd already grated cheese into a bowl and spread a couple of frozen pastry squares with tomato paste and crushed garlic.

"Pizza? Yum." She stole a piece of cheese and popped it into her mouth. He smiled without looking up from the chopping.

"I didn't ask if you have any allergies. And do you eat meat?"

"No and yes. Right now I think I could eat a horse."

"Haven't got one of those, sorry. How about some nuts?" He pushed a bowl of cashews in her direction before heading back to the fridge and pulling out a package of pepperoni. Nessa settled herself on a stool at the breakfast bar and watched him tear up the pepperoni before sprinkling the cheese, meat, and vegetables on the pizza.

"What would you like to drink? We're not quite as well-stocked as your bar, but there is some very nice wine."

"Sounds good," Nessa agreed. "Red, if you've got it."

"Sure." He pulled a bottle from a small wine cabinet set into the kitchen counter, opened it, and poured into what she was pretty sure was a Riedel crystal wine glass. Accepting the glass gingerly, frightened of breaking something which probably cost nearly as much as she made in a week, Nessa took a sip of the wine.

Her eyebrows flew up. "Please tell me you have permission to open this stuff."

"Free rein of everything in the house." Jace shrugged. In truth, the wine he'd opened for her was probably the least expensive one he had on hand. The wine cellar under the house had much more expensive ones stored in a climate-controlled vault.

"In that case, I shall appreciate every drop. Since it's probably my only chance ever to drink wine this good. It's Grange, right? What vintage?"

He put the bottle down in front of her silently, kicking himself for not having thought to pick up a cheaper bottle when he was at the resort. She was a professional bartender; of course she knew her wine. "Enjoy. I'm gonna go have a shower while the pizza cooks. It won't be long."

*   *   *

Jace was acting a little odd, Nessa thought as he left her alone. Picking up her wineglass, she headed over to the open doors leading out to the pool. Maybe he was a little nervous? She was pretty much a sure thing, after their scorching hot kiss earlier. Surely a guy who looked like Jace didn't lack for women throwing themselves at him, especially in New York. She hadn't asked what he did, but he had to be pretty successful if he ran in the same circles as people who could afford to own a holiday house like this.

With a little sigh, she propped one shoulder against the doorframe and sipped her wine, feeling the cool afternoon breeze blowing lightly over her warm skin. She wore nothing beneath her dress, and looked forward to shocking Jace with that fact.

"Hey," Jace's voice was soft as he approached her from behind.

Nessa smiled but didn't turn around, feeling his hands curve gently around her waist as he bent his head to kiss her bare shoulder. One thin spaghetti strap had slipped down onto her upper arm, and his fingers grazed her skin lightly as he lifted it back into place.

"Hey yourself." She set her glass down on the small table just inside the door and turned to look up at him. His shaggy blond hair was still wet, dampening the collar of the crisp white dress shirt he'd put on but not buttoned. A drop of water ran down the center of his muscled chest, and she couldn't resist the impulse to lick it off.

Jace's hands came up, one to cradle the back of her head, the other under her chin to tilt her face up to him. His mouth slanted down over hers and this kiss was even better, even hotter, than the one they'd shared on the boat.

Nessa found herself pressed back against the doorframe, her arms coming up to wrap around Jace and hold him closer. One of his legs thrust between hers and she moaned into his mouth, grinding against his muscled thigh. Her nipples pebbled, pushing at his chest through the thin cotton of her dress. He brought one hand up to palm her breast, grazing his thumb over the aching bud.

Putting her hands beneath his shirt and stroking at his back, Nessa moaned into Jace's mouth when he pinched her nipple. Lifting one leg, she hooked it around his thigh to try and pull him closer still, not that there was the slightest space in between them. He lifted his mouth from hers only to kiss down her neck, nipping and licking at her throat, his tongue tracing hotly into the delicate hollows of her collarbones.

"Jace." Her voice was a husky rasp, a plea.

He took it for a request to stop, though, and moved back reluctantly, his hands falling away.

Nessa grasped at his shirt. "Take me to bed."

He looked down at her for a moment, a muscle in his jaw bunching and releasing, before nodding. "Let me turn the oven off."

It was a good thing he'd remembered, Nessa thought as he went into the kitchen and flicked a switch before returning to her side and offering his hand, or they'd probably have burned the house down instead of just burning up the sheets. At the very least, they would have stunk the kitchen up with burned pizza. She tangled her fingers with Jace's and let him lead her back to the bedroom, then draw her over to the beautiful bed with its silken sheets.

Nessa's long braids swung around her shoulders as she reached down to grasp the hem of her dress, drawing it up and over her head in one smooth movement, revealing she wore absolutely nothing underneath.

"Holy moly," Jace breathed, standing back to take her in. She stood unselfconsciously, comfortable in her nudity, aware of her own feminine power. Her breasts were high and full, tipped with plump nipples which were almost black on her dark brown skin. A narrow waist flared to gloriously curvaceous hips and down to juicy thighs, which he'd been thinking about having wrapped around his neck since he first saw her in her spectacular red bikini early that morning.

"You are stunning," he said reverently.

She smiled at him, chin lifted high and proud. "Get naked," she ordered, and he shrugged hastily out of his shirt, fumbled at the button of his shorts, watching lustfully as she turned her back on him and slid onto the bed, sighing luxuriantly as she lay down on the silk sheets. "Ohhh, this bed is even more comfortable than it looks."

Jace couldn't get out of his clothes fast enough, almost tripping as he kicked off his shorts. His cock stood up stiffly, leading him toward Nessa's lush body laid out on his bed, wanting to worship her.

She beckoned to him with a finger, smiling as he moved to the end of the bed and knelt at her feet, reaching to lightly grasp her ankles. "And what are you planning to do down there?" Nessa asked, hoping she already knew.

Jace's smile was lopsided, his eyes hooded with lust as he looked up the length of her body. "I'm gonna eat you all up, gorgeous." Slowly, he licked his lips before bending his head and pressing the first of many heated kisses on her leg. "So just lay back and relax."

Somehow, she didn't think she was going to be able to relax, not with Jace's warm, skilled fingers and his hot mouth working up the inside of her legs, switching from one to the other, nibbling and licking. He started sucking a love bite onto the tender skin of her inner thigh, and the first involuntary moan escaped Nessa's lips.

"If you don't like anything I'm doing, just say so. Or shove me off," Jace lifted his head long enough to say.

"Shut up and carry on," Nessa commanded, her eyes closed.

Jace laughed and obeyed, his fingers sliding further up her thighs. She had strong, muscled legs–he guessed she was on her feet at least eight hours a day in the bar, which required a certain degree of physical fitness even if she did no other exercise. She shivered as he edged higher, goose bumps springing up on her skin; he kissed them, nuzzling at the softness of her inner thighs, tasting her skin. He smelled the salty-sweet tang of her arousal and glimpsed the moisture welling below her neatly-waxed black bush.

As Jace moved higher, Nessa lifted her knees, spreading her thighs wider, giving him tacit permission to do what he liked. His arms slid beneath her thighs, pushing them up onto his shoulders, his hands reaching to grasp her waist.

"You better hold on tight, beautiful." His voice was lower than usual, a sensual rasp which scraped along her nerves, making her shiver in his hold. "I'm about to rock your world."

Nessa's teeth sank into her lower lip. Reaching down, she wrapped her hands around his wrists, holding on as he'd ordered. Jace made a low sound of approval, right before he pressed his tongue firmly against her clit.

Slim fingers clenched on his wrists and Nessa made a hissing noise between her teeth. Her clit was swollen, wet, under his tongue as he worked it over with slow, steady laps. He listened to her breathing quicken, feeling her thighs begin to tremble as they pressed on his shoulders. Patiently, he kept his pace slow, learning the exact pressure and movements to make her squirm and cry out, make her shudder and say his name in a low, husky voice which drove him wild. Grinding his hips against the bed in an effort to contain his own arousal, Jace kept at his self-appointed task until Nessa made a high, keening noise, her whole body tensing up, her hips lifting off the mattress to push herself harder against his face.

He sucked gently on her clit as she came, listening to her gasping breaths. He brought her down with care until she became too sensitive and let go of his wrist to push on the top of his head.

Leaning back and propping his chin on one hand, Jace grinned up at Nessa. "Feeling good?"

She made a vaguely incoherent noise and beckoned at him. "C'mere. Cuddle."

"Sure." He moved up to lie beside her, pulling her into his arms.

She sighed contentedly and reached to kiss him, not minding the taste of her own juices on his lips. Snuggling against him, she held on tightly for a little while. "You're really good at that," Nessa said finally.

"I aim to please."

She giggled at the tone he affected, planting a kiss on his collarbone. "I feel like there's something pressing I should remember, though."

"Yeah?" Jace laughed too. His cock was indeed pressing hard against her stomach, shoving urgently at her even though he wasn't moving.

She hadn't taken a good look yet, so she moved back a little to eye him up. "Mm, hello." He was long and thick, flushed with arousal, pre-cum beading at the tip. Reaching down to take him in hand, Nessa swiped her thumb over the creamy droplet, rubbed it gently into the head of his cock.

Jace made a hungry, eager little sound in his throat. Nessa looked up to meet his eyes and found them closed, his head thrown back. Blindly, he reached out to cup her breasts in his hands, tweaking her nipples, rubbing them between finger and thumb as she stroked his cock.

His attention to her breasts renewed Nessa's arousal, and she reached her free hand under the pillow to grab the condom she'd stashed there after her shower.

Jace opened his eyes as he heard the rip of the packet, smiling to see what she held. "I like a woman who thinks ahead."

She grinned, rolling the condom down over his straining arousal. "Always prepared, that's me."

"Isn't that the Boy Scouts' motto?"

"It's my motto. Call me a boy again and I won't jump your bones and make you scream my name."

Laughing, Jace rolled to his back, letting Nessa climb atop him, straddling his hips. "Trust me, beautiful, nobody could ever mistake you for a boy." His hands described an hourglass shape, tracing the air an inch away from her breasts and hips.

"Good." Grasping the root of his cock in her hand, she lowered herself onto him, guiding him into her wet channel. They both moaned simultaneously as they came together at last, Nessa's hips rolling to take Jace deep inside her body.

He grasped her hips in his hands, bracing her as she set up a rhythm, lifting up slow and then pushing down hard. Jace watched with something approaching awe as Nessa rode him, her head thrown back, long braids swinging around her, breasts bouncing as her strong thigh muscles worked, her body driving him hard and fast toward orgasm. He could feel it coming, the tingle of heat spreading from the base of his spine. Wanting Nessa to come with him, to share the ecstasy, he put a hand between them to rub his finger over her slippery-wet clit.

"Oh God, yes!" Nessa stuttered briefly in her rhythm, before resuming it again. She leaned forward to kiss Jace, sloppy and desperate as the tremors raced through her body, making her breasts tingle and her thighs shake. He held her close, working over her clit, his other hand cupping and squeezing her ass. Her nipples brushed against his chest, the final stimulation to push her over the edge, and she wailed his name against his lips.

Jace roared wordlessly as Nessa tightened around him, the hot wet clamp of her pussy sucking his climax from him. His eyes closed, his body shuddering as his seed jetted hotly deep inside her clutching, willing body. Stars burst behind his eyelids with the utter bliss of the release.

They clung together for several long minutes, breathing fast, skin damp with exertion. Finally Nessa pulled back slowly and flopped down on the mattress beside Jace, moving closer to press her cheek against his side as he held an arm out toward her. He hugged her close, enjoying the way she fit against him.

It had been a long time since he'd felt so relaxed and comfortable. Tired from the day's exertions, he wanted to stay awake, to savor every moment of being with Nessa, but his eyelids felt incredibly heavy. *Just a few minutes*, he thought as they drifted closed.

CHAPTER SIX

Nessa knew the exact moment Jace fell asleep. Already relaxed, his whole body went limp, his breathing slowing even further. Smiling, she stayed cuddled up to him for a little while, until her stomach rumbled loudly. So loudly, she feared she might wake him up.

Grinning, Nessa eased out from Jace's arm and climbed off the bed. Picking her dress up off the floor, she put it back on and headed for the kitchen to see if she could rescue the pizzas. They weren't fully cooked, so she took them out of the oven and switched it back on again before retrieving the glass of wine she'd abandoned. It was too good to waste. Sipping it as she waited for the oven to heat back up, she looked around the open-plan area with interest. The furniture was minimalist, glass and chrome, but looked expensive. The couch was white leather and a painting hanging above it looked vaguely familiar. Narrowing her eyes, Nessa stared at it for a long moment. It looked like a Georgia O'Keeffe. And she had a sneaking suspicion it was an original.

Well, the house had very clearly been built with no expense spared. The kitchen appliances were top of the line and she was pretty sure the gleaming tiles on the floor were Carrara marble. An O'Keeffe original just fit with everything else. Obviously Jace moved in some pretty exclusive circles.

Sipping her wine and walking around, Nessa peeked through an open door to see a lavishly equipped office, with three computer monitors on one desk. Stock market feeds scrolled silently across the screens.

She'd never asked what Jace actually did, she realized, but a stockbroker made total sense, all things considered. Some sort of commodities trader, maybe. He'd certainly have wealthy friends in that world and be accustomed to the finer things in life, like expensive wine. No wonder he hadn't blinked at opening a $500 bottle of Grange. He probably drank pricier wine every night in New York.

A photograph on the far wall caught her attention. She glanced around, feeling a little like an intruder, before taking a step into the office to look more closely. *The door was open*, she justified to herself.

The photograph was of a woman, slim and fair-haired, smiling into the camera. A baby was held in her arms, as fair and smiling as she was. From the fashion of the woman's clothes and the quality of the image, Nessa thought the picture was maybe thirty years old, but not much more than that. It was taken in Sydney, that much was clear; the distinctive shape of the Opera House was visible in the distance over the woman's left shoulder.

A ping from the kitchen startled her and she hurried back to find the oven was ready. The pizzas would only take a few minutes to finish off, so she figured she should wake Jace. He was tired, but he needed to eat to refill his energy reserves.

"Hey." Sitting on the bed beside him, she shook his shoulder gently. "Wake up, sleepyhead."

"No," he grumbled, an arm snaking around her waist to pull her back down beside him. "Don't wanna."

Laughing, she wiggled to get free, digging her fingertips into his ribs to tickle him. "Come on! Food's ready and now I'm really starving."

He groaned and let her up after stealing a kiss. "Alright, I'm coming!" Yawning, he stumbled after her into the kitchen and found himself pressed to sit down at the dining table while she dished up the food. "Hey, this isn't right. I invited you to dinner, why are you doing the work?"

"Because you fell asleep on me." She brushed a kiss against his temple before sitting down beside him and reaching for the salad she'd quickly thrown together.

Jace looked guilty. "Sorry about that…"

"I'm not offended." Nessa smiled at him to show him she meant it. "It's obvious you're not quite up to peak condition yet, Jace. I'd probably have fallen asleep myself after that spectacular sex, except my stomach was rumbling too loudly to let me!"

"You thought it was spectacular?" He looked almost shy, like he was desperate for her approval.

Putting down her fork, Nessa leaned over to kiss him, slow and sensual. "Damn right, and once we've eaten I'm fully planning to take you back to bed and find out just how good it can get."

"I am very much on board with that plan." Jace smiled at her as she pulled back and picked up her fork again.

"Eat up your vegetables like a good boy then, and I shall think of a suitable treat to give you afterward."

Shoving a deliberately large mouthful of salad into his mouth, he grinned around it as she laughed at him.

*   *   *

Nessa woke in the morning light, stretching luxuriantly. Every muscle in her body ached, but in the best possible way. Jace lay sprawled on his back beside her, the sheet tangled around his lean hips. A beam of sunlight slipped past the blinds to cross his chest, turning the hairs there to burnished gold. Fast asleep, stubble beginning to sprout on his cheeks, he was easily the most beautiful sight Nessa had ever awakened to.

Honestly, she'd like nothing more than to wake him up and carry on where they'd left off late last night, but the angle of the sun told her she'd already slept long past the time she needed to be up and moving. Slipping quietly from the bed without waking Jace, she found her clothes and pulled them on with a wrinkle of her nose; she'd have to move quickly to get back to her room and have a shower before she needed to get to work. Bending down, she brushed a light kiss over Jace's cheek, but he never even stirred. She crept out with a fond smile back at him. No doubt he'd stop by the bar later. Maybe she'd let him take her out to dinner this time.

*   *   *

The pool bar was busy that morning; a large group of new resort guests had arrived the previous day and set up camp. It was a wedding party, Nessa soon discovered, almost thirty young people who were close friends of the bride and groom. They kept her busy serving beer and cocktails from shortly after she opened the bar, too busy to dwell much on the events of the previous day other than feeling the pleasurable ache in her thighs and groin whenever she moved.

It was about two o'clock which she spied Jace arriving; he raised his eyebrows at the crowd around the bar, but found himself a stool at the far end in the shade and waited until she had a moment for him.

"Hey." Nessa dropped a coaster in front of him and smiled. "Sleep well?"

"Better than I have in a long while." Snagging her hand, he dropped a quick kiss on the back of it. "I can see you're busy, angel. Don't worry about me."

"'Kay. Get you a drink?"

"I wouldn't say no to a mojito."

She smiled and reached for the fresh mint stored in the cool box below the bar. "Coming right up."

Nessa had served Jace his drink and was busy making a pitcher of margaritas for the bride and her friends when, from the corner of her eye, she spied Luke walking up to the bar. She wasn't worried about the resort manager dropping by; Luke was a hands-on type and regularly did a walk-around of all the different facilities. She usually saw him at least once a week, and indeed when she was really busy he wasn't averse to rolling up his sleeves and helping serve drinks. He cocked an inquiring brow at her now.

"Need a hand?"

"I'm good, thanks." She gave him a cheerful smile, handing off the pitcher to the drinks waiter. "Get you anything?"

"I could go for a ginger ale," Luke grinned back at her, turning to survey the happy, noisy crowd around the pool as Nessa scooped ice into a glass and topped it off with the amber fluid and a lime wedge.

"Your wish is my command. Hey, I think we need another keg of Carlton Dry; are there any up at main stores?"

"I'll check." Luke pulled his phone from his pocket and tapped in a message before picking up his drink and toasting her. "Cheers." His gaze slid past her, and a broad grin spread across his face. "Hey, Jace!"

Surprised, Nessa turned to watch as Luke rounded the bar to greet the other man. The expression on Jace's face was oddly panicked.

"I didn't know you knew Luke," she said.

"This guy?" Luke jerked his thumb at Jace's chest. "I hope you've been taking good care of him, Ness. One word from him and even I would be out of a job."

"Don't be ridiculous," Jace said weakly.

"Sure, sure, you know you'd never find anyone as good as me to run this place for you. Trust me, you'll never find a better bartender than Nessa, but since you're drinking one of her creations, I guess you already figured that out."

Luke chuckled, placing a friendly hand on Jace's shoulder.

Nessa's jaw had tightened, her lips thinning as she clamped them together. Obviously not trusting herself to speak, she turned away with a curt nod to pour more drinks as her server returned.

"Fuck." Jace shut his eyes and groaned.

"Why do I have the feeling that I just completely put my foot in it?" Luke asked, glancing from Jace to Nessa's turned back and the tightness of her shoulders. "She didn't know who you were?"

"No…"

"And that's a problem because…"

"We've kind of been seeing each other."

"Shit, Jace." Luke blew out his cheeks, shaking his head. "I'm sorry."

Jace shook his head too. "No, it's okay. I should have told her who I was. I knew no good was gonna come of keeping the secret, but it was hard to know what to say."

"Yeah, because 'I'm a billionaire and my family owns this whole island' is kind of a big thing to hit people with right off the bat." Luke's mouth twisted. "I really am sorry. Nessa—well, clearly you've already clued in that she's special. Would you like me to speak to her?"

"Oh hell no! I clean up my own messes, Luke. It wasn't your fault, you had no way to know I'd been misrepresenting myself. No hard feelings." Jace smiled to show Luke he meant it, but he never took his eyes off Nessa's turned back, her tightly controlled movements which spoke of her tension and upset. "I think I'd better give her some space."

"That's probably a good idea unless you want to get brained with a vodka bottle. Want to come for a walk with me?"

"Also probably a good idea." Getting up, Jace cast one more look at Nessa's turned back before following Luke. "So, where are we going?"

"Marine biology labs. They've got a rescued dolphin in the big pool and have been treating cuts on her fins after she tangled with the props on a fishing boat."

Jace couldn't help but think of the day before and Nessa telling him she'd like to take him to meet the marine biologists and view the facilities. It was more than possible that would never happen now.

"Sure," he said finally. "Lead the way."

CHAPTER SEVEN

Nessa tried to ignore Jace, but every fiber of her body was aware of him walking away with Luke, of the way he kept looking back at her until they were lost to sight behind the palm trees.

How in hell had she misread him so badly? How had she not picked up the fact he was hiding such a huge secret? Even more importantly, why was he hiding his real identity?

Thinking back, she realized Jace had never actually told her his surname. He'd never asked hers, either. *Could I need any more proof that I'm just a fling?* Disgusted with herself, she broke a glass washing it with unnecessary vigor. Swearing under her breath, she carefully cleaned up the shards and dumped them in the trash.

"Yeah, yeah, I'm coming," she told the waiter coming back to the bar and waving frantically at her. *No time for self-pity now, Nessa. You've got a job to do.*

The bar was busy until her seven o'clock closing, and she had a lot of work to do to close up. It was almost eight when she finally got to the staff dining room to find some dinner. Cory and Olivia waved her over to eat with them, but she shook her head, in no mood for company, finding a quiet table for one near the back of the room. She finished eating quickly and headed back to her cabin, just wanting to be alone.

There was a figure sitting on the steps leading up to her small veranda. Moonlight glinted off blond hair. Nessa stopped in her tracks.

"This is a staff-restricted area," she said, finally finding her voice. "Although I suppose that doesn't mean much if you own the entire fucking island."

Jace winced at the fury in her tone, then got to his feet. "Nessa…"

"You *lied* to me." Stepping closer, she jabbed a finger into his chest. "You told me the villa was owned by a friend."

"Well, technically it is--"

"Yeah, because you and your father are friends, right?" She shook her head. "Don't pull that on me, Jace. I can understand why you didn't blurt it out the first moment we met, but once you'd asked me out and I said yes? You should have come clean."

"I should've."

Nessa blinked, surprised at his calm agreement. "Why didn't you, then?" she demanded fiercely, still spoiling for a fight.

"Because you treated me like a normal person. Like just another guy who hit on you at the bar, and it was amazing."

"What? You get off on being shot down or something?"

"No, it's not that. I'm just… so used to being treated as one of *those* Hunters, looked at as some kind of meal ticket, that being treated as though I'm just another guy… it was unique, refreshing. As are you. I didn't want things to change, Nessa, and I knew you'd look at me differently if you knew I was rich."

"You're so dumb!" She shook her head at him. "I already knew you were rich; you run in circles with people who own private holiday villas worth tens of millions of dollars. I figured you for a Wall Street guy, the kind who gets seven or eight figure bonuses a couple of times a year. It makes no difference to me if you're a millionaire or a billionaire; I knew you'd be gone in a few days and I'd still be here, because I'm not the kind of girl who would ever be seen in society on your arm."

"Why not?" He sounded genuinely confused.

"Because I'm black and I'm from the East End of London, which is the wrong side of the tracks no matter how you cut it, and I don't want to be some sort of Pygmalion figure! I'm happy being who I am, Jace. I've made my choice and built myself a life I like; if I want to have a brief affair with some guy who will be gone in a few days, that's my choice too. You, though, you're not just any guy. Word gets out that Jace Hunter is on Sunfish Island dating some black chick and the next thing you know there'll be paparazzi lurking in the shrubbery outside my room trying to take nude photos through the goddamn window!"

He winced again, and Nessa shook her head. "I didn't sign up for that, Jace. When were you going to tell me? Were you ever, or were you just planning to leave and never let me know the truth?"

"I hadn't thought that far ahead. I just… fell for you." He stood still, hands hanging limply by his sides. "I never meant to lie to you. Certainly not to expose you to unwanted attention from the media or anything like that."

Nessa just stared silently at him for several long moments. "I can't do this right now," she said finally. "I'm sorry, Jace. I'm just… not in a place where I can deal with this right now." Walking past him, she unlocked her door.

"Can we at least talk about it?"

"About what?" Turning to look at him, she shook her head. "About the fact that I would never have said yes to a date with you if I'd known who you were? What the hell were you thinking, asking a girl like me out, anyway?"

"What do you mean, a girl like you?" Jace asked, baffled. "You're smart, beautiful, sassy; I'd have asked you out if I met you in a bar in New York instead of one here."

"Even if I was working behind it?" Nessa asked cynically.

"Yes! God damn it, Nessa, I'm not a snob. I don't care what background you came from, what matters is the person you are now."

"A bartender. The billionaire and the bartender, sounds like a Lifetime movie--"

"Stop putting yourself down!" He took two quick steps to stand right in front of her and reached up to grasp her shoulders. "You're not inferior to anyone, Nessa. Not because of your chosen profession or the color of your skin or any other damn thing. You'd slap me silly if I dared to imply that you were, so stop doing it to yourself, and while you're at it, don't treat me differently because of who I am. Money doesn't make anyone special, regardless of how some people seem to think it does."

"Don't be naive! You wouldn't even be back here if it weren't for the fact that you own the damn island!"

"I said it doesn't make me special, not that it doesn't buy me special treatment. I'm just a man, Nessa. The same man who made love to you last night."

His words stirred an instinctive reaction from her as her body remembered all the delicious things they'd done to each other the previous night. She looked away, unwilling to meet his eyes.

Jace's hands dropped from her shoulders. "I'm sorry I didn't tell you the truth," he said quietly. "I just… liked the way you looked at me. The way you talked to me. I didn't want that to change."

"It's changed now," she said, and regretted it immediately when he took a step back.

"Yeah. I guess it has."

There was silence between them for a tense, stinging minute, and then Jace said, "Look, I'm not gonna harass you. You know where to find me. Maybe you can sleep on it and we can talk tomorrow."

"Maybe," Nessa said finally. At least he was putting the ball in her court, giving her the choice; she was pretty sure he wouldn't turn up at her bar.

"Good night, Nessa." Jace's voice was soft, tender. She hardened herself against the impulse to tell him not to go, to grab his sleeve and drag him into her room, to her bed.

"Good night."

*   *   *

A knock on the villa's front door at nine o'clock the following evening had Jace falling over his own feet, desperate to get to the door. Yanking it open, he didn't bother to restrain his groan as he came face to face with Luke.

"Expecting someone else?" Luke asked dryly.

"Hoping. Not really expecting." Jace stepped back, gesturing for Luke to come inside. "Want some coffee?"

"Sure." Luke eyed Jace critically. "You look like you've been up all night."

Jace didn't answer, just leading the way to the kitchen and pouring a cup of coffee for Luke. "What brings you here?"

Accepting the cup, Luke leaned back against the kitchen counter and took a sip of the aromatic brew, eyeing Jace over the rim. "I got a visitor this morning. If it's any consolation, I don't think Nessa got any sleep either."

That didn't sound promising. Jace sighed. "She doesn't want to see me, does she?"

"She asked if she could take some holiday days," Luke said. "Girl hasn't taken a vacation since she got here. I said she could go as soon as I could rustle up a cover roster for her bar, which will probably take me until the end of the day. Highly likely she'll be on the boat to Airlie tomorrow morning, so if you want to talk to her, today's your chance."

For a moment, he was tempted; he considered going straight for the door and rushing over to the resort to find Nessa. Reason won out, though.

"She's doing this to get away from me. Going to find her would be a pretty shitty thing to do when she's clearly trying to escape." The words burned like acid in his throat, but he made himself accept the truth. Nessa wanted to get away from him. He wasn't about to force himself on her, not now and not ever.

Luke studied him in silence for a minute before nodding and setting down his cup. "I'm sorry I dropped you in it," he said, "but you should have told her the truth from the beginning."

"I know."

"Good." Luke nodded curtly. "You might be my boss, but I can't have my staff harassed, Jace. Thank you for doing the right thing."

"No hard feelings," Jace said honestly. None of this was Luke's fault; indeed, he respected the other man more now, because Luke had obviously come here willing to stand up to him for Nessa's sake, even knowing Jace could fire him on a whim. "I'm glad she, and all your other staff, have someone who's willing to be in their corner." He offered his hand to shake. "And tell Nessa… well, tell her if she wants a holiday, that's great, but she doesn't need to leave because of me. Sunfish Island is her home and I don't want her to feel uncomfortable here. I'll stay a day or two longer, but I'm feeling a lot better now. It's time I got back to work."

Luke accepted his hand and smiled. "I'll let her know, but I'm gonna encourage her to take a few days. She could use a break. And let me know before you head out, yeah? It's been good getting to know you."

"You too." Jace was coming to think of Luke as a friend, he realized; even though Luke had known his identity from the beginning, he'd still treated him as 'normal'. Would Nessa have done the same, if he'd given her the chance?

He'd never know, now. Bleakly, Jace admitted to himself he'd absolutely blown it, as Luke took his leave and departed, the door closing behind him with a final-sounding thud. Nessa didn't want to see him, was even making plans to get away from Sunfish in order to avoid him. Whatever dreams he might have been harboring for the two of them were now dead in the water.

Picking up the phone, he made a call, arranging for one of the Hunter Enterprises private jets to pick him up at Hamilton Island Airport the following morning. He might not head back to New York yet, but he was sure he'd find something to do at the Sydney offices to keep his mind off the broken, shattered pieces of his heart.

CHAPTER EIGHT

"What the hell do you think you're doing?"

Jace looked up in surprise at the yell and smiled at his father. "Working."

"You're supposed to be relaxing in the sunshine," John Hunter said gruffly, crossing the office and reaching to pull his son into a hug as Jace stood up. "You're still too damn thin, though at least you've got some color back in your face. Why'd you leave Sunfish?"

"It was just time, Dad. I hadn't been to the Sydney offices in a while, figured I'd drop in and see how things are here." He smiled through the open door at the anxious PA hovering outside and waved her off before closing the door. While he'd left orders he wasn't to be disturbed, he'd hardly expected his father to turn up.

"Humph." John scowled. "Why didn't you tell me?"

"Because you'd probably have ordered the pilots not to pick me up, and I'd have had to get a commercial flight. Which would be boring." Jace grinned.

"You're not too proud to fly commercial."

"No, but I didn't want to deal with anyone who recognized me asking why."

John grunted again, but Jace could tell he was already forgiven. "So talk to me about the island. How did you like it?" John grabbed a bottle of water from the refrigerator hidden in an antique wooden cabinet and took a seat.

"It's beautiful," Jace said, knowing the word was inadequate. "And the setup is magnificent. I met quite a few guests and nobody had a single gripe. The staff are absolutely on top of customer service, going above and beyond to make everybody happy. I was incredibly impressed with Luke Collyer."

"Good man, that." John nodded in agreement.

"It was really nice," Jace said, thinking it through for the first time, "to be in the middle of one of our businesses, for once. On the ground floor, seeing how the service gets delivered to customers. The staff at Sunfish, they're the heart and soul of that place. They're the face Hunter Enterprises shows to customers, and I gotta say they're doing a hell of a job."

John cocked his head curiously, listening to Jace's impassioned words. "You really liked being there, huh?"

"Yeah." More than liked, he'd loved it. He'd felt comfortable there, for the first time in a long time. The staff on Sunfish were down-to-earth, not afraid to get their hands dirty, hardworking people with a genuine love for what they did. They were far removed from the high-society crowd of New Yorkers who'd been Jace's social circle for the last few years. The mere thought of returning to that sterile, artificial life repulsed him now, and he knew he had to say something.

"Dad—even though I'm feeling better, I don't think I want to go back to the New York office. I… don't think I want to take over Hunter Enterprises from you. Ever."

To his complete astonishment, his father smiled broadly. "Took you long enough to figure that out."

Jace's jaw dropped open. "What?"

"Oh, you could do it, and you'd do it damned well, but you'd hate every minute of it. You're not ruthless enough, son. I love you more than I've ever been able to express, but you've got your mother's heart. God rest her soul."

Jace could hardly believe his ears. He'd always been afraid of disappointing his father, had always striven to be someone John could be proud of. "What will you do with the company?" he asked, almost afraid to hear the answer. "I don't want you to run yourself into the ground with it." It was a large part of the reason he'd worked so hard to be able to step up, knowing John wasn't getting any younger.

"I'm gonna privatize the company. The market's ripe for an IPO, we'll list forty per cent of the stock initially and see how things go. I'll put twenty percent in a trust for you and your heirs; Hunter Enterprises will always look after you, but it was my dream, not yours."

Jace was too choked up to speak.

John reached out to grab him into a tight hug. "I'm damned proud of you, son. Always will be. But you gotta find your own dreams to follow."

Father and son embraced for several long minutes, and John's voice was husky when he finally pulled back and said, "So what's your plan?"

"I don't know, yet." Except he rather thought he did. "I think I'd like to go back into architecture."

"You did graduate top of your class when you got your degree, and God knows Hunter Enterprises can always keep you in work even if you don't take on any other clients." John smiled a little mistily at him.

"I think I'd like to design houses rather than commercial premises, though." Spending time in the villa he'd designed as his graduation project had made him think more about the ergonomics of design, about marrying beautiful design with a home that was easy to live in and maintain.

"The only thing I have to ask you is that you keep everything on the down low until we've taken the initial stock offering to market." John gave him a serious look. "There are a fair number of our senior staff, folks who've been with us a long time, who have a stake in the company."

Jace knew most of the people his father was talking about. He'd grown up around them, called them uncles and aunts, absorbed the business of Hunter Enterprises by learning from their expertise.

"It's only right to do our best to make those shares worth as much as possible," Jace agreed. "Of course, Dad. You can count on me."

"I know." John clapped a strong hand on his shoulder. "We're taking Hunter Enterprises straight to the top of the Dow Jones."

"Just one thing," Jace said. "That twenty percent share you're putting into a trust? Could it maybe include complete ownership of Sunfish Island?"

"Of course." John looked at him curiously. "Sunfish is pretty special to you, eh?"

"It's a pretty special place." He wanted to make sure nobody else could ever come in and impose their own wishes on the island, sack staff and change the guest relations policies that gave the resort such a special atmosphere. Wanted to make sure no matter what, that Sunfish would always be Nessa's refuge.

"It's yours. Forever. I'll make sure of it," John promised, no further questions asked, for which Jace was grateful.

*　　　*　　　*

The news that Hunter Enterprises was going public sent shock waves through the staff at Sunfish Island. They all worried about what it might mean for their jobs, at least until John Hunter phoned Luke personally and told him Sunfish Island was being specifically excluded from the sale.

"Ownership of the island, the resort and everything to do with it has already been transferred into a trust, the sole beneficiary of which is Jace, at the present time, though any heirs of his will also be included at a later date."

After getting his breath back, Luke had to ask why.

A rich chuckle answered the question. "Seems he fell in love with the place, wanted to make sure no corporate types could come in and ruin it. He has ultimate say over anything that happens on the island now—and he asked me to let you know that he has full confidence in you." John paused to let that sink in. "You impressed him, Luke. He'll be in touch soon to let you know that himself, I'm sure, but we're both up to our eyes at the moment, as I'm sure you can imagine. He's in London right now."

Luke was still in a certain degree of shock. "This is so unexpected, Mr. Hunter, but thank you so much for calling to tell me in person. I really appreciate it."

"You're welcome. Don't know what magic you're working on that island but Jace came back a changed man, determined to follow his own dreams. If it was something you said to him, thank you."

"I… don't think it was me."

"No?" John asked curiously.

Luke said nothing.

There was a brief silence on the line, and then John said, "There was a girl, huh? Jace wouldn't talk about it, but I read between the lines."

Luke rubbed his forehead, wondered how much he should say. "He didn't tell her who he was. I accidentally dropped him in it, and she didn't take it well."

"Ahh," John said. "Well, whoever she is, she made him take a good hard look at himself, and he realized he didn't like the path he was on. I must ask you to keep this particular tidbit quiet, but after the stock goes to market, Jace is stepping back from his role here. Going back to architecture, and I have to tell you, I couldn't be happier for him."

Thanking John, Luke ended the call and sat dumbfounded in his office chair for several minutes, thinking through the implications of what he'd just learned. At last, a broad smile on his face, he pushed himself to his feet. The staff would all be relieved to know their jobs were safe, but there was one person he really should tell first.

*   *   *

Nessa had taken a few days off after she broke up with Jace, but knowing he'd left the island, she found herself returning sooner than she had originally planned. Dropping back into her usual routine, she still sometimes found herself looking at the seat he'd always taken at the end of the bar, wishing he was there, looking at her with those steady blue eyes. She'd asked herself a thousand times if she'd done the right thing in ending their relationship.

"Hey." It was Luke who slid onto the bar stool, smiling at her. "Got some news."

"You're not saving it for the staff meeting?" She wiped up a small puddle of spilled soda on the bar with a rag, but couldn't avoid meeting his eyes. It was quiet today, and she had no customers to tend to.

"Thought you might like to hear it first. Turns out Hunter Enterprises no longer owns Sunfish."

"What?" Nessa's jaw dropped. "It's already been sold—before the share offer? Who's the new owner?"

"Jace Hunter."

The cloth she'd been using to wipe the bar fell from nerveless fingers. "Jace?"

"Got the news from John Hunter himself. Jace apparently wanted to make sure Sunfish was safe from any corporate meddling. I've been assured he has complete faith in my ability to run the place… though I'm pretty sure there's one particular staff member I daren't fire."

Nessa found herself clinging to the edge of the bar to hold herself up because her legs felt too shaky to support her. "He did that for me?"

"Pretty sure you're a fairly large part of his motive, yeah." Luke eyed her sympathetically. "You know," he said in an apparent non sequitur, "Olivia still knows a hell of a lot of New York movers and shakers from her days as a marketing guru in the Big Apple."

Nessa eyed him curiously. "So?"

Luke grinned. "So, I have an idea."

CHAPTER NINE

Nessa smoothed her hands over the skirt of her orange silk dress once more, before stepping forward and handing the printed invitation she held to one of the PAs manning the door into the massive ballroom. Olivia's friend had assured her the invitation was completely legit, but Nessa still had the terrible feeling the PA, a beautiful blonde with a snooty expression on her face, would dismiss her as a fraud and probably have her arrested.

"Your name is Tennessee Williams?" The blonde gave her a skeptical look. Nessa cursed the last-minute rush which had meant Olivia had to email her friend a copy of Nessa's passport in order to get the invite organized in time for the event.

"Blame my mother, and please, please just call me Nessa," Nessa replied.

The blonde actually chuckled. "I know just how you feel. I'm Donna… but my real name is Chardonnay."

They exchanged conspiratorial grins, and Donna found Nessa's name on the list on her tablet and checked it off. "Have a good evening... Nessa."

"Thank you, Donna." Taking a deep breath, she tightened her grip on the fashionable little clutch Olivia's friend had provided, along with the designer dress and heels, before moving through the huge doorway into the ballroom.

Luke's brilliant idea had been for Nessa to fly to New York and use Olivia's old contacts to wrangle herself an invitation to the special Hunter Enterprises post-IPO party. Nessa still wasn't entirely sure how they'd managed to talk her into it, but here she was, wearing a dress worth more than a month's salary and a pair of shoes which probably cost as much as a new car, despite each apparently consisting of little more than a couple of flimsy straps, some rhinestones, and a sharp heel.

There had to be five hundred people here already and more arriving by the minute. How was she ever to even find Jace, never mind get close to him? She'd arrived in New York early that morning and spent the day being pampered in a ridiculously high-class beauty salon before coming here, but she'd taken the time to check the stock market. Wall Street was going crazy over the offering, the stock already soaring to almost five times its initial list price. Everyone here tonight looked to be celebrating pretty hard.

"Nessa?" a voice said behind her and she startled, spinning around and almost tripping over her heels. A slim Chinese woman in a designer business suit stood there; agelessly beautiful, her eyes told Nessa she wasn't nearly as young as she might be mistaken for.

Who the hell knows I'm here? "Um, yes, I'm Nessa."

"I thought you might be. I'm Nancy, Jace's assistant."

"He knows I'm here?" Nessa fought the urge to panic.

"Actually, he doesn't." Nancy reached out, giving her a gently reassuring pat on the arm. "Luke called Mr. Hunter–Mr. *John* Hunter, that is–and let him know you were coming. John asked me to be on the lookout for you."

"Oh." Nessa's shoulders relaxed a tiny bit.

They tensed right back up when Nancy said, "I can take you to Jace now, if you'd like?"

"I think maybe I need a drink first. Liquid courage and all that," Nessa admitted.

Nancy smiled, beckoning to a nearby waiter. "After the chaos this last week has been, I wouldn't say no myself. Champagne?" She scooped two crystal flutes off the waiter's proffered tray and handed one to Nessa. "Cheers."

"Bottoms up," Nessa said with a smile in return. The champagne was fabulous; Cristal, she was pretty sure, though the glasses were pre-filled and she couldn't see a bottle.

"Don't go anywhere," Nancy warned the waiter before draining her glass, handing back the empty and taking another one. "Come on, Nessa, keep up," she chided.

Laughing, she decided she rather liked Nancy. Nessa followed suit and claimed another glass. On an empty stomach, the bubbles went straight to her head, making her feel floaty and relaxed.

"Okay," she declared, "I think I can face him now."

"Marvelous." Nancy linked her free arm through Nessa's and drew her through the crowd. She seemed to know almost everyone there, greeting many people by name but forging an inexorable path onward until the last group of people melted aside and Nessa saw Jace.

Wearing a pale gray suit perfectly tailored to his tall, lean form, his blond hair immaculately cut, his jaw clean-shaven, he looked every inch the billionaire.

Right down to the famous supermodel on his arm, laughing as he spoke and leaning in to press a kiss on his cheek, dangerously close to his mouth, leaving a scarlet imprint of her lips behind. A camera flashed to capture the moment and the group surrounding Jace laughed, knowing what picture they'd see in the society pages of the papers tomorrow.

Nessa froze like a deer in headlights, staring as Jace turned his head to speak to the other woman. His gaze passed over her briefly, unseeingly. But that was enough. She yanked her arm from Nancy's and spun on her heel, rushing through the crowd as fast as she could manage in her narrow-skirted dress and ridiculously high heels, blinded by the tears running down her cheeks.

*   *   *

"Nessa?" It took a moment for Jace's weary brain to process what his eyes had just seen; his gaze snapped back to the woman he'd spotted in the crowd. She'd already pulled loose from Nancy and turned away, running through the crowd, long black braids swinging behind her.

Yanking his own arm free from the woman trying desperately to cling to him, Jace rushed forward. "Was that really Nessa?" he demanded of Nancy, waiting only for her nod before sprinting after Nessa's disappearing back.

She'd come. She'd come to him. Only to arrive just as some fortune-hungry attention-seeker tried to sink her claws into him. He could only imagine what Nessa must have thought of what she'd just seen.

The crowd slowed him down, stockbrokers high on champagne and success trying to catch onto him, shouting their congratulations, demanding to know where he was going in such a rush. He ignored them all.

"Nessa!" he yelled, losing sight of her briefly. Damn, she was quick even in a dress and heels; he pulled loose from the hands grabbing at him and raced after her. "Nessa!"

By the time he reached the doors, she'd disappeared. He looked frantically around, wondering which way she'd gone.

"Did you see a beautiful black girl in an orange dress run past?" he begged the PAs at the door, all staring at him as though he'd lost his mind.

"Nessa?" Donna, one of his junior assistants, asked. At his nod, she continued, "She went that way." She pointed to the hotel's main doors leading out onto Fifth Avenue.

"Bless you!" He followed at a dead run, but reached the exit just in time to see a cab pull away from the curb. "Damn, damn, damn!"

"Mr. Hunter?" Turning, he found Donna behind him, her expression anxious. "Is everything alright?"

He took a deep breath. "No."

He knew Nancy had trained the girl well when her expression smoothed to steely resolve, her chin lifting.

"Tell me what you need, sir."

*　　*　　*

The only good thing about her hasty dash home was when she'd boarded the flight still in her designer dress and heels, the check-in agent had taken one look at her outfit and given her a free first-class upgrade. The plane had been halfway across the Pacific when Nessa finally gave in and cried. A concerned flight attendant promptly descended on her with tissues, chocolate, and alcohol, which at least made the interminable flight seem to pass a little faster, even though she couldn't sleep.

At last, she stepped off the late afternoon boat from Hamilton Island and headed for her cabin, feet dragging with weariness. Falling face-down onto her bed still in her designer finery, she fell into blissful unconsciousness.

A loud rapping on her door woke her up. Groaning, Nessa pushed herself off the bed and headed for the door to open it.

"Oh. It's you," she said to Luke. Holding up a hand to forestall whatever he was about to say, she told him, "I don't want to talk about it. I just want to get back to work, okay?"

Luke shrugged after staring at her in silence for a moment. "Fine by me. It's nearly ten, though. Are you working today or is Eric covering the pool bar?"

She'd slept for almost sixteen hours! Startled, Nessa nodded. "I'm working." Looking down at herself, realizing she was still wearing the designer gown, she said, "I'll just take a shower and head on down there."

*   *   *

It felt good to step behind her bar again, even if her bottles were all in a muddle, she saw as she unlocked the grille covering them and pulled it back. Shaking her head, she started sorting them out. Why on earth was the Bacardi on the top shelf? She used it every five minutes making cocktails. Putting it back front and center in its usual place on the lowest shelf, and beginning to sort the other bottles, she whirled around as a voice said, "Hey, Nessa."

It couldn't be… but it was, it was indeed Jace, leaning on the edge of the bar, wearing his old T-shirt with the sleeves ripped out, his sunglasses pushed on on top of his head, a good day's worth of stubble gracing his jaw.

The gin bottle Nessa was holding slid from nerveless fingers and hit the rubber mat at her feet, fortunately not smashing. She stood rooted to the spot, eyes on Jace, unable to believe what she was seeing.

"Don't be throwing the booze around, now." He straightened up and came around the bar, picking up the gin and putting it back on the shelf. Turning back to look down into Nessa's stunned face, he pleaded, "Say something, Nessa."

"What are you doing here?" she asked numbly.

"I'm home."

"What?"

"This is home, now. The villa is, anyway. I'm no longer working for Hunter Enterprises; I'm starting a private architecture consultancy and design business, based right here."

She couldn't make a sound come out, but her lips shaped the word, "Why?" and Jace understood.

"Because of you. You made me see that the life I was living was slowly killing me, that I had to make a change, find what I really wanted and go after it. This is what I really want to do, Nessa, and you," he lifted a shaking hand, tracing a finger gently down her cheek, "*you* are who I really want to be with. No high society lifestyle, just you and me and the things that make both of us happy."

"The girl I saw you with in New York…?"

"I'd just met her and she clamped on like a leech. I couldn't ditch her fast enough. I still can't believe you really came." He was still touching her, his hand curling around the back of her neck to draw her closer. "I barely got a glimpse of you, but you looked amazing."

Nessa laughed shakily. "I felt a fool. I didn't fit, there."

"You fit with me, and that's all I care about. We were both square pegs in round holes in our old lives, but put two square pegs together and you get… a really nice rectangle… okay, that analogy fell down a bit there."

"I like rectangles," she said nonsensically, but Jace's smile lit up as though she'd said three quite different words, and maybe in a way she had.

"I like rectangles too," he agreed, drawing her closer and bending his head until their lips met in a thoroughly satisfying kiss.

~ The End ~

ABOUT THE AUTHOR

Caitlyn Lynch is an Australian author who loves writing about sexy people finding their happily ever after together!

You can connect with her on her website

www.caitlynlynch.com